Will was starved. All he could thi... ...was *food!*

He was scrambling, clawing, and scratching over the backs of others like him, anxious to get to the grub.

LEMME AT IT-LEMME AT IT-LEMME AT IT

Suddenly, Will stopped.

Glancing down at his hands, he saw the same terrible claws the other raptors displayed. On his feet, something clicked and clacked—retractable crescent-shaped hooks, powerful and deadly.

Will shuddered. "My name is William Stuart Reilly," he whispered. "I am a thirteen-year-old *human.*"

He felt his tail swoosh from side to side.

HUNGRY-HUNGRY-HUNGRY-HUNG—

"I don't care if I'm hungry," he hissed. "I'm not—" Something hairy and ratlike poked its head out of a tiny hole. Will roared and leaped for it!

Long before the universe was ours... it was theirs!

Don't miss the first two DINOVERSE adventures by Scott Ciencin

#1 I Was a Teenage T. Rex
#2 The Teens Time Forgot

And look for these titles coming soon:

#4 Please Don't Eat the Teacher!
#5 Beverly Hills Brontosaurus
#6 Dinosaurs Ate My Homework

DINOVERSE

RAPTOR WITHOUT A CAUSE

by Scott Ciencin

illustrated by Mike Fredericks

Random House 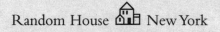 New York

To my incredible wife, Denise.
Every moment I spend with you is precious—
all of time itself would mean nothing to me without you.
—S.C.

Text copyright © 2000 by Scott Ciencin
Interior illustrations copyright © 2000 by Mike Fredericks
Cover art copyright © 2000 by Adrian Chesterman

www.randomhouse.com/kids

Library of Congress Catalog Card Number: 99-67550
ISBN: 0-679-88845-4
RL: 5.5

Cover design by Georgia Morrissey
Interior design by Gretchen Schuler

Printed in the United States of America May 2000
10 9 8 7 6 5 4 3 2 1

Dear Reader,

Welcome to Book #3 of DINOVERSE!

You may wonder if the age of dinosaurs was anything like what you're about to read. According to the fossil record, it very likely was. How did the dinosaurs live? What did they eat? What about the weather and landscape? All of those questions have crossed the minds of scientists. And the fossil record has given the answers to them, to me, and now to *you*.

If you've read the first two books in this series, you've already seen Bertram Phillips's weird science fair project in action. The device zapped the minds of Bertram and three other Wetherford Junior High students into the bodies of dinosaurs. Bertram and his friends had more than a few wild adventures before returning to the present. But the story is far from over.

Unknown to Bertram, his science teacher has spent the last eight months tinkering with the M.I.N.D. Machine. Now some extreme things are about to happen to a whole new collection of Wetherford students. Bertram may be their only hope of returning from the predator-infested swamp that is prehistoric Texas. Can he guide them through the perils of ravenous raptors, cataclysmic weather, and a mystery that may change all of history?

To find out, come back with me to a time when the world belonged not to humans but to the most magnificent creatures the Earth has ever known.

Scott Ciencin

Psssst! Want to make a dinosaur roar? Flip the book's pages and keep your eye on the dino in the lower right corner.

And be sure to check out Bertram's dino notebook on page 185.

Wetherford, Montana
Mid-May, 7:40 a.m.
Four hours and forty-one minutes
to Time Displacement Event

Will Reilly stared up at the T. rex.

The sun shone behind the dinosaur, casting its massive form in a brutal silhouette. Its powerful teeth glistened. Its claws were moist with dew.

"Isn't this a *great* morning?" Will asked. He pulled a single flyer from the armful he carried and stuck it on the sharp bronze claw of the statue. It fluttered in the early morning breeze.

Will pulled his emerald baseball cap lower, his rich blue eyes hidden by mirror shades. All that was visible were his perfect cheekbones and the tiny cleft on his chin.

He turned and smiled as his best buddies Lance and Percy crossed the school lawn.

Lance was bigger and broader-shouldered than Will, with a scar over his left eye from a motorbike accident the summer before. His hair was so black it was Superman blue.

Percy looked small and frail next to him, his red hair his only exceptional feature. Though Percy was short, he was also the fastest runner on Wetherford's track team—ever.

"What's the latest?" Will asked as he poked Lance's shoulder.

Lance did a little hip-hop step as he took the flyers from Will. He was the best dancer in the entire school. "Me, Lisa Garvey, the party, *tonight*."

"You're kidding."

"Nope. Wore down her defenses."

Percy looked at the flyer. "Hey, this says—"

"Victory party tonight!" Will chuckled, handing Lance and Percy their own stacks. "A chance to celebrate with your newly elected Freshman Class President!"

Percy's eyes widened. "But—they're not announcing the election results until first period. Shouldn't we *wait* before we start putting these out?"

"It's a lock," Will said. "No one's gonna vote for Cal Myers. He's only been here three months."

"Yeah," Lance lifted a fist. "Solidarity, man!"

"Sure, sorry," Percy said.

Will tapped a campaign pin attached to his

RODMAN 32 tank top. "Class President two years running. Go with what you know!"

That had been Will's campaign slogan. He slipped his hands into his baggy jeans and looked around. The lawn was filling with students.

"We're on," Will announced. His pals nodded.

As one, they turned from the statue of the giant dinosaur that Bertram Phillips and his dad had discovered earlier in the year. They all knew the drill. Not just *anyone* got invited to Will's parties. And it was up to Will to make the natural selections.

As he sauntered toward the school, Will was mobbed. With a nod or a flick of his wrist, Will let Lance and Percy know who should get an invitation.

A cute seventh-grade girl with dark, curly hair walked by, her head down.

"Her," Will said.

Lance blinked in surprise. "Do you know who she—"

"Do it."

When Lance handed her an invitation, her pretty green eyes lit up.

"Are you serious?" she asked. Wearing a bulky sweater, black skirt, and out-of-fashion green boots with four-inch platforms, she wasn't the type who usually graced Will's parties.

"Come on. Have a good time!" Will said.

With a shriek of delight she ran to her friends.

They all looked at Will in awe. He loved the attention. The power.

And school was the one place where he could have it.

"You eat that stuff up," Lance said. "And man, do you have an appetite!"

"Hungry-hungry-hungry," Will said. "That's me."

Inside Will and his pack prowled the halls, handing out flyers.

Monique Dombrowski, the captain of the girls' basketball team, sauntered their way. She was the hottest and most popular girl in the eighth grade. Her raven hair and long, tanned legs were heart-stoppers.

"Does this mean I'm your date?" she asked, fanning herself with the flyer. Monique was surrounded by a pack of her own. Monique the Man-Eater.

"You're *something*," Will said playfully.

"As if I didn't know *that*." Monique floated away.

Lance looked at Will. "So, Bruce Wayne, how does it feel to be a millionaire playboy and the most sought-after bachelor at Wetherford?"

"Shut up," Will said, thinking, *it feels great—and it's gonna feel even better next year!*

"Zane's been missing all morning," Lance said, changing the subject.

"Bet he's working on the Secret Mission," Percy said.

"*That* makes me feel all tingly," Will replied. "I—"

A loud crash came from just ahead.

Will pushed through the crowd to find Leiman Crews slamming Zane against his locker.

Leiman was lean and muscular. He wore a white Armani shirt, and his Rolex sparkled in the overhead light.

Zane McInerney was Leiman's opposite. He was roundly built, with warm eyes and big elephant ears that he'd spent years trying to learn to wiggle.

Inside his open locker were photos of comedians and props for some of Zane's sight gags.

Zane lived for the spotlight, though Will was sure this particular spotlight was not what he had in mind.

"What'd you think you were doing?" Leiman bellowed.

"Hey, Leiman!" Will cried, shouldering aside a group of eighth-graders. "Lay off!"

Leiman turned to reveal cold, dark eyes and a predator's smile. "I keep forgetting. This belongs to you, doesn't it?"

Leiman dropped Zane as if he'd been handling something distasteful. Zane's face flushed with shame.

"What's the problem?" Will demanded, getting into Leiman's face.

"A little prank," Leiman shot back. "It's not that I can't take a joke. I just won't take it *from* a joke."

"Someone welded his locker door shut!" Zane cried, his voice filled with panic. "I can't weld! I flunked shop!"

"It was probably J.D.," Will said, referring to J.D. "Judgment Day" Harms—a thug with no neck, brains, or conscience. Wetherford's most cruel and unusual.

Leiman sneered and turned to Zane. "Boo!"

Zane jumped. Everyone laughed.

Leiman was about to saunter off when a foot hooked his ankle and a shoulder slammed his upper body. Leiman hit the floor with a thud.

His attacker stood above him. It was Patience McCray, a rising star on the girls' basketball team.

"Oh, I must not have been looking where I was going," she said innocently, running her hand through her long light-brown hair. "I guess you were beneath my notice or something."

Leiman rose and looked over her oversized sweat-shirt, jeans, and dirty Nikes. "Accidents happen," he hissed. "Especially when people forget to take out the trailer trash."

As Leiman went by, Will stepped forward.

"*I'm* impressed," he said, offering her a flyer.

"Happy for you," Patience said, as she vanished into the crowd.

"Whoa," Lance cried with a shiver. "*That* was cold."

Will nodded his head. But he really *was* impressed.

The bell for homeroom sounded. Percy rushed off. Zane filled the opening at Will's side.

"Leiman?" Will said. "Who names their kid Leiman, anyway? That guy's such a jerk." Will paused. "I wonder if my dad was like that."

Zane saluted. "Ah—your dad! Briefcase Man! Able to balance large checkbooks and buy—"

"Sell!" Will hollered.

"*Buy!*" Lance countered.

"—entire manufacturing firms in a single bound!" Zane continued. "And, with his special Briefcase Man powers, nothing sticks to him! His force shield repels all attacks!"

"That's my dad. Don't wear him out," Will said, thinking about his father, who spent his whole life chasing after wealth and power. That wasn't the life Will wanted. He liked to enjoy himself!

"Update on today's events," Zane announced. "After your victory this morning, you can rest assured that the bell from our local Taco Bell was successfully acquired at oh-two hundred hours and is, even now, sitting in Vice Principal Kadophski's VW."

"Cool," Will said.

Lance handed Zane some flyers. "Give these out, okay?"

"Uh—yeah, thanks, you're welcome," Zane muttered.

Lance turned to Will. "What an idea! That's the way to get people talking about you."

"*My* idea," Zane said softly. "But that won't matter unless someone needs to do time. Well, the goldfish in the principal's office know me by name. They'd miss me if I didn't make regular appearances."

Lance patted Will on the back. "How do you think this stuff up?"

"Natural talent," Zane said with a shrug. "So I hang around with you guys and people don't see me as a loser."

"And you don't get the stuffing kicked out of you by morons like Leiman."

"Yeah," Zane said. "That, too."

As they slipped into Mr. London's homeroom, Lance took the lead, crying, "Make way for your Class President!"

Will was greeted by a round of applause. The audiovisual guys were already setting up. The announcement would be made right here during first period. It was the only class Will and his presidential opponent shared.

A beautiful blonde wearing a tight sweater and a short skirt appeared before Will.

Candayce Chambers.

"We need to talk about the fund-raiser for the children's hospital," said Candayce. "You said we'd start planning it two weeks ago. Any of this sounding familiar?"

"Sure!" Will replied. "Just a lot going on. The

election and all." He jammed a flyer into her hand.

"Come to the party," he said. "Don't worry so much."

"It's my job to worry," she said with a frown. "We talk tonight. I mean it."

"Whatever," he shrugged.

Zane whimpered as Candayce sashayed off. "I want, I want. Gimme, gimme..."

"I heard that!" Candayce said over her shoulder.

Other students flowed into the classroom, including Cal Myers and Leiman.

Will tried to get a look at his competitor, but a pack of students converged on him. Cal's blond curls and sculpted features were hidden behind his admirers.

Two suits stood at the front of the room. One held a microphone.

Principal Matthews cleared his throat, and the sound looped back through the P.A. system. Mr. London, their homeroom teacher, stood beside him. The principal looked at Mr. London's tie, then shook his head.

Principal Matthews had the same sour look Will's dad usually sported.

"Principal M!" Will cried. "Can we get a shout-out?"

Everyone laughed. The principal gave a slight smile and shook his head *no*.

Even a tiny smile from Principal Matthews was a

major achievement, and Will was proud of himself.

The bell rang and everyone took a seat. Leiman snagged a chair next to Will.

"Thought we should talk," Leiman said.

Will didn't look at him.

While the principal looked on, Mr. London started class. "I have the feeling that this morning your minds are elsewhere," he began. "So we should run with that."

He opened a briefcase and took out the latest issue of *Incredible Tales*. A dinosaur was on the cover.

"How many of you have read Bertram's latest Dinoverse adventure?"

Groans could be heard as nearly every hand was raised.

"That's good, considering it's required reading." Mr. London smiled.

Students liked Mr. London because he was a lot like them. For one thing, his suits were usually jazzier than the stuff favored by the other teachers. And today, his pink Energizer Bunny tie *made* the look.

"You're all familiar with the basic idea," the teacher continued. "A young man builds a M.I.N.D. Machine that takes him and his friends back in time and into the bodies of dinosaurs."

Mr. London paused.

"If such a machine existed, a machine that could

place your mind within the form of anyone, or any-*thing*, throughout the history of this planet, past, present, or future, where—"

The principal cleared his throat and gestured toward the door.

"One moment," Mr. London said. He and Principal Matthews went into the hall and appeared to be arguing.

"My dad says Mr. L's not coming back next year," Leiman said. "He hasn't been sticking with the curriculum. Acts like he's teaching college or something. And ever since that little snot Bertram and his dad found that dinosaur, all London's got is dinosaurs on the brain."

"What do you want?" Will said, facing Leiman.

"I think I've got you figured out." Leiman leaned closer. "I kept trying to figure out why you even acknowledge their existence."

"Who?" Will demanded.

"You know who I mean," Leiman replied. "There's us and there's *them*. But you don't know the difference between being popular and being elite. Let me put it another way."

Will hoped Mr. London would come back soon.

"It's like the Greek gods," Leiman continued with a smirk. "When you're popular, you're one of the gods. Everyone else is a worshiper. Get it?"

Will focused his eyes on the front of the room.

"Now," Leiman sighed, "gods *need* their worshipers. They'd fade away without them. So, sometimes the gods get involved with mortals. They have to. But being one of the elite is better."

"Really," Will said. He didn't want to hear this.

"When you're elite, it's like you have wings. You're not depending on anyone or anything to hold you up."

Leiman paused and shook his head sadly. "But when you're just popular—being treated like a god—you're still depending on others to keep you up there. And what happens if they go away? Without wings, you fall."

Will sighed. "That was fascinating, Leiman. But what do you really want?"

"Just to get you thinking," Leiman said, the smirk in place. "My friends and I think you should be one of us."

"You want me to come over to the dark side?"

"That's not how I would have put it," Leiman replied. "I just want you to know there's a place for you, no matter what happens."

Leiman settled back in his chair as Mr. London and the principal returned. Principal Matthews tapped the mike.

"This is it," Lance whispered.

Will nodded, easing himself back in his chair. He didn't want to look *too* eager.

"Good morning," Principal Matthews said. "I'm here in Mr. London's natural science class to announce the results of the election for Freshman Class President."

Will lowered his shades and smiled as the principal took out an envelope and tore it open.

"The students of Wetherford Junior High have chosen—"

Will started to get out of his seat.

"—Cal Myers!"

Will froze. His smile didn't fade. He didn't move. Couldn't move.

"Cal, why don't you come up and tell us what you have to say?" Principal Matthews offered.

Cal shrugged and walked to the front of the class.

Will felt a hand on his shoulder. "Clap," Lance said.

Will clapped mechanically, his smile firmly in place. But Will's skin felt clammy and a prickling sensation rippled down his arms and legs.

Soon everyone was clapping, and ignoring Will, who slunk into his chair.

Cal took the microphone and shook Mr. Matthews' hand.

"Three months ago, I was new here. I didn't know anyone," he said. "Now I want to thank everyone for letting me get to know you, and for giving me your votes. Here's to the future!"

Principal Matthews actually smiled. "Well said."

Then the bell sounded and it was time to head off to the next class. Will and Lance were the last to leave, along with Cal. Leiman approached, holding one of Will's flyers.

"What do you think, Cal?" he asked. "Are you swinging by Will's victory celebration? It is in *your* honor, after all!"

Cal held out his hand to Will. "Thanks for clapping," he said. "You made things a lot easier!"

Will clasped Cal's hand. It was warm and strong.

"Listen," Cal said, "I could really use an adviser. What do you think?"

Lance stepped between them. "We'll get back to you."

"Yeah!" Leiman called. "And Will—don't forget to get back to me, too!"

In the hall, everyone stared. Will was surrounded by an army of curious, staring *eyes*—eyes peering at him as if he had transformed into something alien and unknowable.

"Keep smiling," Lance said.

What had just happened? Will wondered.

Lance shook his head. "You. An adviser. Can you believe that guy?"

At least it would be something, Will thought.

"Listen," Lance explained. "You've got classes. I've got classes. This is where we split up. But there's something you've got to think about. Okay?"

Will nodded.

"Stop smiling, you look like an idiot."

Forcing the muscles in his face to relax, Will drew a deep breath. "Okay."

"We've gotta do what Briefcase Man would do. Turn a negative into a positive. We've invested too much to let it all end here. We've got to fight back."

Will felt dazed. "What are you talking about?"

"You *lost,* but it doesn't mean you're *defeated,*" Lance continued. "We need to come up with something that'll take everyone's mind off this. Something so big that when people talk about this day, they're not even gonna *remember* the election. But it's got to be something perfect. Something spectacular."

"You think that's possible?" Will asked.

Lance grinned. "You know what Mr. London would say. If you can imagine a thing—"

"You can make it a reality," Will finished.

"I'm going to come up with something. Do you believe me?"

"Sure," Will said. He raised his chin. "Absolutely."

Lance punched his arm and took off. Will turned to face the staring crowd and the rest of the morning.

*Six minutes and forty-six seconds
to Time Displacement Event*

Will sat at his usual table in the lunchroom, waiting for his friends. He hadn't eaten. He had no appetite.

Usually, if he was sitting alone, it didn't last for long. Other students would soon gather around. But not this morning.

Leiman took the seat across from Will. "So, are we still in the denial stage, or are you mad yet?"

"Mad at who?"

"Them. All of them," Leiman said with a wave of his hand. "Your worshipers let you down. I mean, they used you for target practice."

Will wished his buddies would show. He could walk away—but his was *their* table. He wasn't giving it up. And Leiman had a point, as much as Will hated to admit it. He'd done a lot for the student body over the last two years.

"Move off," a voice said.

Will looked up to see Lance standing above Leiman. Zane and Percy were with him. They carried full trays.

With a shrug, Leiman rose. "At least you'll always know where you stand with us. It'll be with your back to the wall, but at least there won't be any surprises. See ya!"

Lance nearly spilled the contents of his tray as he

slammed it to the table. "Do *not* listen to him."

"How'd he know?" Will asked. "It was like he knew I was going to lose before it even happened."

"That's not why he's been hanging around," Lance said.

Will scratched his head.

"That girl with the curly hair and glasses you invited to the party?" Lance continued. "That's Leiman's half-sister. He tries to pretend she doesn't exist. You made him lose face."

"Okay..."

"Damage control, stage one, has begun," Lance said, his voice lower. "Percy's got new flyers printed, and all three of us have been passing them out. Pretty much everyone's been going for the rethink."

Will nodded. "That's great."

A sudden commotion made them look up. The girls' basketball team swept in from practice. They were completely transformed. Gone were the sweaty jocks and intense players. In their place came a gaggle of girly-girls. They wore makeup and skirts and heels, while their jewelry jangled daintily.

Then came Patience, still wearing the same baggy clothes she always wore. Her backpack was slung over her shoulders.

"Hey, Patience!" Monique called. "Got a date for the party? No, waitaminute. While we were discovering boys, you were discovering layups."

Tanya Call laughed beside Monique. She ran her polished fingernails near her face like they were claws, then fanned them with a predatory motion. "Naw—she'll be too busy pumpin' iron, gettin' ready for her days on the boys' wrestling team."

"Face it," Monique declared. "The whole tomboy thing is sad. A little work on the hair, the makeup—"

"The clothes," Tanya added.

"Yeah, all that," Monique nodded. "Then you will look like an ugly *girl* instead of—whatever!"

All but two of the girls laughed.

Vicki Gallagher and Mindy Margolis, two of the most popular players—and girly-girls through and through—joined Patience. All three shook their heads and went off to eat lunch together.

Will saw Zane smiling broadly as he checked his watch. "Now things really get interesting. Observe."

As if on cue, dozens of guys leaped to their feet and raced to Monique, waving sheets of paper. They were the lowest of the low of what Wetherford had to offer. Too skinny, too fat, too uncoordinated, too plain, too tall, too rude, too nasty, too *unacceptable* ever to have a chance with Monique.

"I got the right answers!" one of the guys cried.

"Me, too!"

"Yeah, and me!"

They crowded around her, while Monique batted at

them and tried not to get swallowed. Finally, she shrieked and ran screaming from the cafeteria. The guys followed.

"Win a dream date with Monique Dombrowski," Tanya read from one of the sheets of paper. "Answer the following questionnaire and check your results against those posted on Anonymous_Rex.com."

Someone laughed out loud.

"If you're a winner," Tanya continued, "be the first to give a printout to Monique at exactly twelve eighteen and you will have her heart—and more."

"The Secret Mission," Will whispered. "I forgot!"

Lance tapped Will's arm. "Check out Patience."

She was laughing louder and harder than anyone.

"Now on to stage three," Lance said. "Listen closely..."

Two minutes later, Will asked for a word alone with Patience. A copy of the magazine with Bertram's story in it lay open before her. The illustration showed a young man standing in front of an incredible machine, tendrils of energy engulfing him.

"Did you like the bit with Monique?" Will asked.

Patience's smile faded. "Why?"

"It was a present. For you. I figured you'd like it more than flowers."

Will hated lying.

Her eyes narrowed. "Guys don't get me presents."

"Come on. You've been in the newspaper, on TV, I've seen you at parties." Will poured on as much charm as he could.

Patience lightened up a little. "What do you want?"

He told her his plan.

Patience remained impassive through his entire pitch. Then she sat back and shrugged.

"So, this wouldn't be like a real date?" she asked.

"No, of course not!" Will assured her.

"You and your buddies would take me out after school, whip out your parents' credit cards, and get me a wild dress, a makeover, whatever I want?"

Will nodded.

"Then we show up at your party tonight and everyone keels over. Especially Monique."

"That's it!" Will said, smiling.

"And people are, like, 'Whoa, Will Reilly tamed the savage beast. The girl who tried to burn down the orphanage when she was eight, who put Larry Sommers in traction when he grabbed her butt. And here's Will, who turned this hard-core heinous witch into the beautiful princess. What a guy!'" guessed Patience.

"Well..." Will didn't see how Patience could resist. It was the perfect plan.

"You perform this legendary stunt that'll make folks forget about the election, and I get turned into the pretty woman everyone just *knows* is inside wait-ing to get out. And they all think you transformed me overnight, right?"

Will relaxed. He had her.

"Yep," he said. This *would* be spectacular. He wanted this so much. Needed it. *Hungered* for it.

Patience looked away.

Suddenly, Will felt odd. His skin grew cold and prickly. And though he was indoors, he thought he felt a wind kicking up, an electrical charge in the air.

He clutched at his head as a vision burned itself into his brain. A vision of Mr. London standing before the M.I.N.D. Machine, the one from Bertram's story, only—only it was real! "I can see any age. Any time," Mr. London said in the vision, as he worked the machine at a fever pitch.

Then the image was gone. Will knew he was los-ing it big time. This was like something from Bertram's story!

He turned to Patience. "What do you say?"

Patience smiled as she balled her hand into a fist. "That I've never been more insulted in my life."

She hit him hard, just as a streak of blue-white lightning shot up from the floor. As Will fell, the lightning struck out, changing directions, leaping over students. Finally, it zeroed in on Will.

Strange energies engulfed him. He saw streaks of lightning rip outward from his hands. One struck

Patience, another Zane, another—he didn't see...

The floor seemed to disappear. Will saw Mr. London. Lightning surrounded him. The machine from Bertram's story rocked and quaked at his side.

Suddenly Will was free. He felt lighter than he had ever felt before, almost like a creature made of dreams, thoughts, and desires. Not a person, something less, and something more—

He heard Mr. London scream, "Dinosaurs! Why—"

Then Will heard a wild yipping, the chattering of teeth. He felt a blistering heat, and—

He was somewhere *else*.

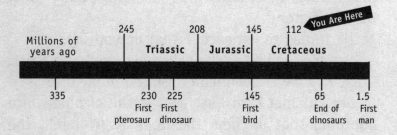

PART ONE

BRAVE NEW RAPTOR

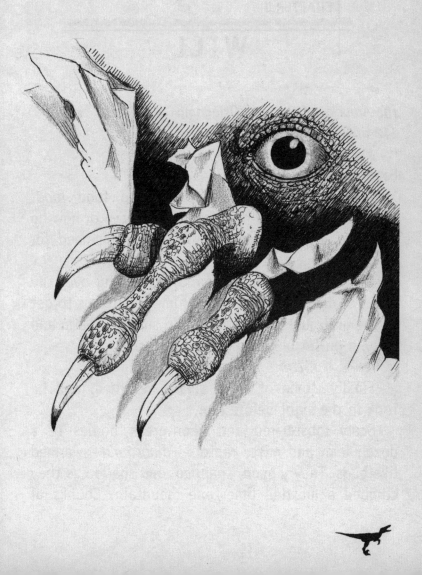

CHAPTER 1

WILL

The Arbuckle Mountains, Oklahoma
112 million years ago

Feeding frenzy!

All Will could think about was food, food, *food!* He didn't care where he was, what he was, or how he got here. His brain was on fire with the need for *food!*

He was scrambling, clawing, scratching over the backs of dozens of others like him, all anxious to get to the grub just ahead. Will could smell it. Warm and juicy, a buffet of rich aromas and tastes.

LEMME AT IT-LEMME AT IT-LEMME AT IT...

Finally, some of Will's smarts returned, and he took in the sight before him.

Scaly lobster-red and neon-green bodies of a dozen lean and nasty raptors—*dinosaurs*—swarmed like bugs. They yipped, snapped, and snarled as they climbed a mottled limestone mountain. Chunks of dirt and falling rock bounced off their bone-hard heads. Claws sliced the air. Tails whacked and whipped. And bellies rumbled.

Will was with the pack. And he wanted food, just like the rest of them!

A raptor struck his back. Its hind claw closed over the top of his skull and the dinosaur vaulted high. Will watched the raptor hop like a kangaroo toward a cave mouth partially blocked by a rock slide. Only a small opening remained.

A raptor with bright blue and pale yellow stripes waited at that gap. He was larger than the others, and Will figured Big Guy wasn't anxious for company—or competition.

Will watched as a raptor tried to slip past Big Guy, toward the hole that was *just* big enough to accommodate his smaller form.

Big Guy stopped the other with a solid head-butt that sent him tumbling down the hill. Will gasped as the *yelping* raptor slammed into him. The impact sent him flying away from the rest of the pack.

Will felt sick as his head hit the rocks again and again while he spiraled helplessly.

He hit the ground hard, his shoulder taking the worst of the impact. Finally, he rolled onto his belly. He lay there, looking up at the mountain.

It was magnificent. The sun blazed just above its peak, and the sky was a crystal blue.

The raptor who'd taken him down was already racing back up the mountain toward the cave and the rest of his cousins. Will could pick him out easily because he was by far the smallest, and he had a bright orange streak on his back. He reminded Will of an overactive puppy.

Go, Binky! Will thought, still dazed. Instinct drove Will to stagger to his feet.

He was hungry. So *HUNGRY-HUNGRY-HUNGRY...*

"Stop it!" Will shouted.

The yelps, honks, and squeals of the raptors were suddenly silenced.

The orange-striped raptor looked at Will. So did the others. Will spotted something he hadn't noticed before. Every single raptor had its front teeth knocked out. Their goofy gap-toothed grins made them look even more crazed and dangerous.

HUNGRY-HUNGRY-HUNGRY

The raptors turned away. Binky scrambled up the mountain while the others tried to unseat the leader.

As Will climbed, his thoughts began to clear. He marveled at the terrible claws that were his hands and the deadly retractable crescent-moon-shaped hooks that clacked on his feet. Will's new body had a striped, rust-colored torso with a splash of sky blue snaking around the belly and legs. He shuddered.

"My name is William Stuart Reilly," he whispered. "I am a *human boy*."

He felt his tail swoosh from side to side.

"I don't want to have scales. I don't want to have a tail. No way, nohow."

His hunger burned. A boiling hot desire that shot through his brain.

HUNGRY-HUNGRY-HUNGRY

"I don't care if I'm hungry! I am not a raptor. I—"

Something hairy and ratlike poked its head out of a tiny hole. Before he could even think about it, Will leaped for it, maw chomping, spittle flying.

But the ratlike thing was too fast. Will dug at the little hole—

HUNGRY-HUNGRY-HUNGRY

—until he could no longer scent the mammal.

Then he knew.

Will looked at the swarming raptor pack, and ran—in the opposite direction.

He raced through a valley with jagged hills all around, filled with trees and lush greenery. Boulders and flowering plants were scattered about.

"I am Will Reilly, Will Reilly, Will Reilly!"

Suddenly, from his right flank, a green and red raptor snapped its jaws in his face. Will tried to dart around it, but the raptor was all over him, slapping the side of his head with its own.

"Ow!" Little pinpricks of light danced before him. Who was this guy? And why did he feel a strange sense of loyalty toward it? Or maybe it was guilt.

"Lance?" Will asked. "Is that you, Lance, buddy—?"

The raptor snapped at him. *Not* Lance.

"Chill, Buddy!"

The raptor hissed. Then he arced his head in the direction of the pack.

Buddy wanted him to go back there!

"Oh, no!" Will said firmly. "Not a chance—"

The raptor kicked him.

The air shot out of his lungs as Will clutched his belly. He found himself staring at the sky.

Buddy shook his head again. Will watched as his sickle-like claw whipped forward, struck the dirt, and latched back.

I have those, too...

Buddy motioned toward the pack and yipped twice. He retracted his claw and raised the foot.

"Okay, okay, I get it!" Will moaned. He still felt dizzy. Buddy set his foot down and allowed his sickle claw to do its thing in the dirt.

TICK-CLACK-TICK-CLACK.

"Don't mess with Buddy, Buddy's been working out," Will muttered as he trudged back to the mountain. Buddy nipped at his heels, and Will picked up the pace. Finally, the raptor bit at Will's aching shoulder. Will broke into a run.

This was a lot like home...

Buddy ran rings around him—literally—and bumped Will a couple of times, just to make sure he understood who was boss. And the closer Will came to that cave, the more he could smell it.

Food. Lots of food. Waiting inside...

Rats, he decided. *Probably a whole family of rats. Maybe hundreds of them.*

"Gahhh!" he gagged at the thought.

But his belly *liked* the idea.

Will found himself climbing. Vaulting. Hopping. Buddy was driving him on like a drill sergeant. But he barely noticed the other raptor. His hunger had put him into overdrive.

Then the pack was before him and Buddy was hanging back. *It's all up to you now!* Will saw Big Guy driving off another challenger.

He forced himself to think. It was difficult because of his incredible hunger. Will studied the large raptor. Stacked up at his feet was a collection of small, ratlike mammals just waiting to be devoured.

But getting at them was the problem. For some reason, Big Guy wanted to see if anyone could get past him and claim the prize.

How many times have I seen this at school? he wondered. <u>*Mano a mano*</u>—<u>*macho a macho*</u>—*and you'd better understand who's boss!*

A raptor Will hadn't noticed before sat to the side of Big Guy, licking his claws and crunching on his morning snack. This one had a red body and amber and turquoise spots.

He was Big Guy's favorite.

Junior. And Junior was getting a meal deal without having to work for it. Just like Cal. Or Leiman...

"Figures," Will muttered. He watched as two more raptors raced at Big Guy and were repelled without effort. Every single raptor used the same failed tactic, and Big Guy seemed pretty pleased with himself for turning them all away.

Will wondered what the bigger dinosaur would do if he were faced with a *real* challenge. "You're not too smart, are ya?" "I like that in a raptor..."

A few of the other raptors ceased their frenzied attempts to climb higher and stared at him.

"You think it's cool when I talk?"

The raptors scrambled away, clearing a path.

"Hey, this isn't so bad." He looked back. Even Buddy was eyeing him intently. Will started singing, then rapping. He was a rappin' raptor.

Maybe it was the music, but in a strange way, Will was starting to feel like he was back on familiar ground. All eyes were on him, and the more he talked, the greater the awe he inspired.

Buddy was impressed. Binky, too. All Will needed now was for Big Guy to let him by and—

A raptor swiped its sickle claw at him. Will jumped, fell over a couple of other raptors, and grabbed a clawful of thick roots to keep himself from sliding down the mountainside.

He saw his mistake. The raptors didn't like it when he talked. It wigged them out!

Buddy came up from behind. A chirpy kind of yipping filled the air. Laughter, he was sure. Were the others *laughing* at him?

That's it, Will thought, moving quickly.

He was getting past Big Guy, to the action. And it wasn't because he was hot for a rat-bake—though, *yuck,* he was—it was because if he got through that passage, which Big Guy was too big to fit into, it would lead somewhere Big Guy couldn't go.

The other raptors would *have* to be impressed.

It was a ploy, just like the one he'd used in the lunchroom with Patience...

Will took advantage of the distraction he'd provided. He launched himself at Big Guy.

His claw scraped along the side of the mountain, and a handful of dry earth was suddenly his. He vaulted over the head of another raptor, and felt like he was flying. This raptor body had power unlike anything he'd ever known!

He landed in front of Big Guy in a cloud of dust. The larger raptor turned and Will tossed the dirt into his eyes. Blinded, Big Guy hissed and fell backward!

All the other raptors wailed in fright. This was their leader. Big Guy! How could anything happen to *him?* And who *was* this masked stranger who had done what no one else could?

Will flung himself at the darkened opening, his maw closing on one of the stilled bodies of the mammals. The moment he tasted his first bite, instinct took over. He felt like he was at an all-you-can-eat buffet and this scrumptious meal before him was all that mattered in the world.

Roars came from behind him.

Will stared down at his claws, felt his tail slap against the walls of the narrow tunnel, and thought of the maddened raptor at his heels. Big Guy wasn't going to let Will take the top rung without a fight. Abandoning his meal, Will pushed deeper into the cave.

His head went through, but his body stuck. Will wriggled and clawed at the rock beneath his belly. As he pushed, the opening grew tighter. Rock fell on him.

For all he knew, the passage led nowhere, yet he *smelled* something. A wisp of cool, fresh air drifting toward him. And something else, something he couldn't identify—

He strained his muscles, pushing and clawing, digging and yelping. He struggled to push on, then something closed on his leg.

Blinding pain shot through him. A terrible pressure squeezed his leg so tightly he thought he might black out. Will smelled the dinosaur behind him, and he knew it was Big Guy! And he wasn't happy.

Junior was his favorite, not Will!

Will lashed out with his foot. He struck something solid. Big Guy's big fat head, Will guessed. Another set of claws was on him, and he was dragged back into the light, kicking and screaming! Will grasped with what had been his hands and came up with a clawful of dead mammals.

FOOD-FOOD-FOOD

Will yelped as the hungry raptor pack climbed over him to get at the food. He was trampled and kicked.

Then a set of claws closed on his legs. He was dragged out of harm's way and came to rest on a teetering rock.

Buddy stood over him, yipping furiously. Nearby, Binky trembled with excitement.

You gotta think of us, man, the pack, the team, we look out for each other—

Suddenly, Buddy leaped into the middle of the feeding frenzy. Binky followed, and the path leading away from the raptor pack was wide open.

But before he could make a break toward freedom, Big Guy and Junior were on him. They sent him flying down the mountainside so quickly the scenery blurred. He landed in the flatlands far below and arose *smelling* trouble.

Junior came up behind Will and slammed him to the ground with a kick.

"Hey," Will muttered. "What's up?"

Junior hissed. His claws extended. SNICK-CLICK-CLACK.

Will didn't want a fight. He didn't know *how* to fight in a body like this one. And he was alone. Behind Junior, Big Guy appeared.

Will scrambled back—and suddenly a familiar crackling sounded. A wind rose around him. Little strands of lightning flared, surrounding him like a cocoon. Junior and Big Guy yipped and fled.

This is good, Will thought. *Mr. London's got the machine under control. He's gonna fix things, he's gonna—*

"GET ME OUT OF HERE!" Will screamed.

A voice thundered in his brain. But not the voice he expected.

"This is Bertram Phillips," the voice boomed. *"I don't know how long I've got, so listen closely!"*

Bertram? But it had been Mr. London with the machine...Then Will thought about Bertram's stories. How it had been a *student's* science fair experiment that had sent the minds of teenagers back in time and into the bodies of dinosaurs. Bertram's machine!

"Things are happening here," Bertram said. *"Things I can't even begin to explain. People are* changing*. The whole world is becoming something so weird I can't describe it."*

Will thought of the story. Of how a voice from the

future had told the group where they had to go, what they had to do if they ever wanted to get home.

It's happening again, Will thought. *It wasn't just a story; it happened for real and it's happening again...*

Bertram's frantic voice persisted. *"It has to do with the past. Where you are right now. Something's happened. Or, I should say, something's <u>going</u> to happen."*

"Bertram, can you hear me?" Will screamed. "Just get me out of here! Just get me out!"

The voice went on, heedless of Will's demands. *"According to the M.I.N.D. Machine, it's going to happen right where you are now, in the Arbuckle Mountains of Oklahoma, in three days' time. But I don't know exactly <u>what's</u> going to happen. It's something big. Something that'll change everything. There are others back there with you. They're stranded in Texas. I'm using the machine to set up a tracking system, so they can find you and help you."*

Others? Will thought. *I'm not alone?*

"There's a key. An amber key. The others have to find it if you're going to get back. You have to solve the mystery and change the past. If you don't, we'll all be—"

The winds and lightning faded. So did Bertram's voice. It was as if nothing had happened.

"Bertram?" Will called. "You can't leave me like this!"

But no voice answered him. Will looked around. The other raptors had been so engrossed in devouring their meals they weren't even looking his way.

Junior snarled, yipped, and kicked a rock at Will. But he wouldn't get any closer. Finally, Junior ran off, yipping and howling back to the feasting pack. Big Guy glared at Will, then followed.

Will was alone as he gazed at the open stretch behind him. He could go right now and no one would stop him. But then—he'd never get home.

An image appeared in his mind. A vision of his human form lying unconscious on the lunchroom floor. It was hazy. Strange shapes and shadows moved around it.

And there were others stranded back here, too.

Who? Will wondered. *How many? And could they help?*

All he knew was that he had to stay. He was the homing beacon. And he was at Ground Zero. For *something*. And there wasn't much time...

"It wasn't this tough for *you* guys!" Will shouted. But the voice of the winds had faded.

CHAPTER 2

PATIENCE

Killeen, Texas

Patience had a blinding light in her eyes, wind and rain on her scalp, and a giant rising up over her.

There was something else. Words. Someone shouting above the wind: *"Solve the mystery and change the past. If you don't, we'll all be—"*

The words had been going on for a long time, but to Patience they were jumbled and meaningless. The crackling energies that had surrounded her faded. A roar hurt her ears, and a craggy, misshapen thing flung itself at her. She saw gleaming eyes, rippling muscle, flashing *teeth*, and fiery pastels and primary colors.

The colors reminded her of something Monique might wear. But—ugly as it was—the monstrosity wasn't one of her teammates made prehistoric. It wasn't even remotely human.

"Gahhh-ahhh!" Patience responded, smelling its rancid breath. She took a step back as the *thing's* skull smashed against hers. She faltered under the jarring impact. Reeling, she got a good look at her opponent.

Definitely not Monique. The creature had scales and a weird, wriggling sail that went all the way down its back. The animal roared and made a quick dart in her direction, then backed away. It paused and studied her.

Patience tried to piece together what she remembered. She'd been in the lunchroom, looking at Bertram's story and talking with her teammates, and Will had come over. Then there was light—and the world had stopped making sense. She'd been lifted out of her body, spun about, and things had gotten weird. *Really* weird...

Just like in the story. She looked down at herself, studying her scaly form, and *knew* what had happened.

Mud and muck sloshed and splattered with every step she took. Insects buzzed close to her ears and swarmed over her mud-encrusted form. Smoke and the odor of charred meat and other rancid smells filled her nostrils. Rage, hunger, and fear raced through her, igniting a fever in her brain.

The area was soggy, humid, and miserable. She heard frogs croaking and the buzz of wasps and dragonflies. Heavy branches and jagged tree trunks rose from the mud. A spattering of conifers no bigger than Christmas trees circled her and the raging *thing* ahead.

The tree behind the monster was burning. She could feel its heat. All the trees were so small...No, the trees looked small because she was so big—as big as a house!

There was something warm and appetizing and very near. Something shuddering and crying and whipping around in the mud below.

"Small small small small small—not so big at all..." came a shrill voice.

Something *human*.

A growl rumbled.

Patience fixed her gaze on the monster staring at her with curiosity. The sailback was another female—Patience could sense it.

And from the voice of the quaking mass at their feet, the other lucky winner of the oh-yeah-you-just-*know*-I-wanted-to-be-a-dinosaur contest was some guy. The sailback was looking to make lunchmeat out of him...

Suddenly, Patience was afraid of what she was feeling. More than anything in the world, she wanted to pounce on the creature in the mud and sink her teeth into it...

"Okay, we can talk about this," Patience said,

scrambling to get her bearings. The monster before her grunted and licked its shoulder where it had been burned by the fire. Its wavering spiky sail flapped about in the hot wind. So did its tail.

The nearby blaze sent searing waves of heat toward Patience.

THUMP-THUMP-THUMP

The rain beat at her, making it hard to think. Drops that glowed like descending jewels of amber fell from the open sky. A summer shower.

Patience studied her opponent more closely. The dinosaur looked a little like a T. rex. It walked on powerfully muscled rear legs. It had a long snout with jagged, crooked teeth. Its arms were short and tipped with long, piercing claws.

But its skull was longer than a T. rex's, almost egg-shaped. Its nostrils were high triangles, and the creature bore a crown of jagged ridges, beginning at the middle of its forehead. The ridge ran back in a V, passing its maddened eyes, disappearing behind its skull. The sail running down its spine wriggled defiantly.

Amber gold puffs of heat hissed from the nostrils of the beast before her.

"It's okay, Number 47," Patience said. Forty-seven was Monique's number on the girls' basketball team. "You don't want to hurt anybody."

Number 47 still looked confused. Hesitant. She

rotated her neck and rolled her shoulders like a prize-fighter. Little bones popped and crunched. A low rumble emerged from her swollen belly. A growl of hunger.

Not a good sign.

A mild whimpering came from the mud.

Now it was clear. Number 47 was her opposing player, and whatever was in the mud below was the basketball—an *edible* basketball they both wanted to turn into lunch.

Patience shuddered. *That's a human being, not something from McDonalds. Get a grip, girl!*

Number 47 growled in warning. Patience responded to instinct and tried to ball her hand into a fist. She was going to slug it out with a dinosaur!

Only—she didn't have hands anymore. Patience looked at her tiny reptilian arms, swollen mud-spattered belly, and gigantic legs. Her torso was covered by a pattern of amber spots in a sea of deep-brown scales.

And nearby lay the little shuddering, salamander-looking dinosaur, still quaking in the mud.

"Everything's so big. Everything's so big but *me*," it squealed. "Find a happy place. Find a happy place..."

Suddenly, Number 47 came at her. Patience roared and slammed into the other dinosaur. The contact was jarring, but it was satisfying and familiar, too.

They wrestled in the mud. Patience grabbed at the animal with sharp claws. She head-butted it until she felt dizzy. She kicked and bruised, clawed and scraped—all the time she was aware of the dinosaur's chomping, gnashing, mashing teeth, its strength, and its confusion.

Number 47's nostrils flared. It looked at Patience with frightened eyes.

A children's song came to mind: *One of these things is not like the other, one of these things just doesn't belong!*

Patience felt a connection. A *pull* that made her think that she and this dinosaur should be allies.

"No way," Patience snarled.

The dinosaur roared and tried to fasten her teeth on Patience's neck. She batted the beast's skull with her own and rolled clear. Mud splashed all around them!

Then that voice sounded again. "Tiny tiny tiny tiny, not big, not me, I'm tiny..."

She knew that voice, but it was so shrill she couldn't place it.

Number 47 was on her feet. Advancing toward the little dinosaur. Patience wobbled, tried to stand. But her tail was in her way and she couldn't get up!

She flopped onto her belly and crawled as fast as she could to the quivering little dinosaur trapped in the mud. It wasn't dignified, but she got there before the sailback. Patience rammed her head into Number 47's legs. The sailback fell back in a splash of mud.

Patience thought of something her cats did, and she pounced on the fallen dinosaur. Maw wide, she fastened her razor-sharp teeth on Number 47's throat.

And froze.

The dinosaur beneath her ceased its struggle. Patience eased off and Number 47 growled. Patience tightened her jaws again and the dinosaur stopped moving. Its eyes darted frantically.

Stay down, Patience thought. *For once I am going to have the last word with you, you little—*

Patience unclamped her jaws—then whacked the dinosaur. Once, twice, a third time—just to make her point.

Number 47 rolled away.

"B-b-b-belly," the little voiced reptile in the mud said. "Belly. Legs under it. Push up. It's how you stand..."

It worked. Patience rose. The sailback did the same.

"You're an—an—Acrocanthosaurus," the little dinosaur whimpered. "And so is she. And I'm so small. Oh, *my...*"

Patience glared at her fellow Acrocanthosaurus. They circled one another warily.

"Show your supremacy," the little voice mumbled.

"Make it clear that she's not getting this morsel—
me—oh..."

Patience put one muddy foot on the small dinosaur
and roared at Number 47. The sailback hissed and
spat.

Patience smiled inwardly.

"Not so much pressure; you don't need to be so
physical!" her *prey* commanded, his voice almost
normal.

Then Patience understood exactly who was speak-
ing to her—and how she had gotten here...

Number 47 turned and ran. Patience couldn't
restrain a victory roar.

The sailback looked over its shoulder and nearly
collided with a tree. It changed course just in time
and went splish-splashing away.

Patience felt satisfied. She pictured herself at a
game, seeing Monique's family staring at her in shock
and disapproval from the bleachers. The Dombrowskis
were such a bunch of two-faced Bradys. All hugs and
smiles and words of encouragement. Monique was
their Marcia. They couldn't see—*wouldn't* see—what
a monster they'd raised.

The Mushnicks, Patience's foster family, never
once came to a game. But that was all right. At least
they never *faked* being interested in the things she
did. They left her alone—and that was how she liked
it.

"So, Mr. London," Patience said, pushing her foot a little harder into the little one's belly. "The machine's real, huh?"

He nodded.

"We're actually dinosaurs."

Another nod.

"But there's a way back. To our own time. Our own bodies." The words Patience had heard when she'd first arrived now became clear. "That's what that voice was all about. Bertram's voice. His message."

The little dinosaur struggled pitifully. Patience removed her foot.

He choked, sneezed, and spat. "Y-yes."

"Only—he knew enough not to mess with the machine anymore. He isn't the one who did this, is he?" Patience guessed.

Mr. London looked away in shame.

Suddenly, Patience felt a weird sensation deep in the core of her being, a pull to leave this place, and quickly. She fought it. She didn't like anyone telling her what to do. Patience had been moved around all her life, and *no one* ever asked her what *she* wanted. And *this* was the worst of all. But the words of her true basketball coach, the hoopmaster named Holiday, came to her:

It's good to get mad, but _use_ that energy. You know what they say about butterflies? That you can't get rid of them, but you _can_ get 'em to fly in formation? What

you've got inside you isn't butterflies. They're hawks.

Make 'em fly and take you where you want to go.

This is Holiday, signing off.

Remember—with me, every day's a Holiday!

Patience knew what she had to do. Stay focused. Stay calm. Worrying about who was to blame wouldn't get her out of this.

Bertram's words ran through her mind. "So we have to find this amber key and get to Will. Any ideas after that?"

Mr. London climbed to a higher patch of earth. "I..." Then the little dinosaur sunk his head into the mud and was silent.

"You don't have a clue," Patience said with a sigh.

The little dinosaur shook his head.

Patience really looked at him for the first time.

The slim-bodied dinosaur looked more like a lizard than anything. It had wide hips, long legs, and little arms. Its face was birdlike, complete with a quivering little beak. Small, pitiful eyes peered up at her. The rain had washed the muck from its flank and Patience could see its true color.

"You clean up—" she began. Then gusts of laughter erupted from her. Her lips rippled and her eyes squeezed shut.

"What?"

"You're so funny looking! You're so small."

Mr. London's shoulders sank. "I know I didn't

adjust well. It appears I'm a Hypsilophodon."

"You look like you'd glow in the dark! You're lime green and shocking pink, and you're *so funny looking!*" She was giddy and she knew it.

"Thank you."

"I can't help it." Patience forced herself to settle down. But she had needed that laugh. "Number 47 was going to eat you and I was hungry, too, and you don't have enough meat on your bones for two of us, so she and I got into it."

"Number 47?"

"The other dino."

"Could we keep off the topic of *eating me?*" Mr. London asked in a quavering voice.

Patience looked away. "The thoughts are still in my head. I don't want them to be there. They're gross, but..."

"I understand," Mr. London said. "You have powerful natural instincts grappling with your human intelligence. You're in the body of the biggest, meanest predator of this age. What you're feeling is natural. The impulses and such. I'm...experiencing...something similar—the desire to run for my life. Reasonable enough, all things considered."

"What do we do?" Patience asked. "Split up?"

Mr. London's tail whipped. "We need to stay together. Remind one another of who and what we really are."

"So we have to keep from going native. That's the first thing. Then we have to get to—"

Once again she felt that urge—that *instinct*—to be on the move. It gave her a direction to follow. Then she recalled that Bertram said he'd give them a way of sensing what direction to go.

"Can you feel that?" Patience asked.

"Yes," Mr. London said. He sounded terrified.

"I guess we'd better get going," Patience said.

She opened her maw, brought it down on Mr. London's quaking form. Doing her best not to hurt him, she plucked him from the mud, tossed him high into the air, and caught him in her small but powerful arms.

He was shrieking at the top of his lungs even after she broke into a run.

Patience ignored him. She was in the zone. Her thoughts were focused, her mission clear. All she had to do was find the others, get the amber key, reach Will, do—*something*—and get back.

How hard could it be?

I guess it depends on who's on the team. We've got Mr. London for brains—once he stops screaming—and me for brawn...

She recalled the other person she had seen struck by lightning this morning. And for the first time that day, she started to seriously worry.

CHAPTER 3

ZANE

Fort Worth, Texas

Zane McInerney knew *exactly* what was going on.

He had awakened in a strange body, freaked out, and denied the evidence of his senses for as long as he could. Then he settled down to accept what he could not change.

He was a dinosaur. A long-necked brontosaurus traveling along a scenic shoreline with a lumbering herd of lard-bellied earth-shakers.

He'd almost become calm when Bertram's message exploded in his mind and freaked him out all over again. Now he felt the pull that told him where to find Ground Zero, Will, and the action.

He was moving steadily in the opposite direction.

Sorry, Will, Zane thought. *But someone made a mistake choosing me. I'm the comic relief! I'll just mess things up for the rest of you. Better I hang out with these guys, and we can meet up later.*

Sure, he felt guilty. Will had protected him more times than Zane could remember. But that had been part of their unspoken deal. Will kept him safe and made him cool by association, and Zane came up with the gags that made Will a legend at Wetherford.

He'd read Bertram's stories. He knew exactly how dangerous and terrifying the age of dinosaurs could be. And he was defenseless. Even if he broke from the herd and went looking for Will, he'd probably get eaten before he could find anyone else from school.

He bumped into another brontosaurus. "Sorry."

Sight was a whole new experience in this body. His brain was registering two very different images that sat side by side with a little blank space in between. Two panoramic views of breathtaking scenery.

On one side, he saw the shore of a great ocean, storm clouds gathered overhead, a drizzle encompassing the endless horizon. On the other, a beach leading up to a wall of lush green trees that stood proud and tall, like sentinels. Everything was flat. There was no depth at all to any of the images.

His neck was stiff! It itched about five or ten feet behind his head. Looking back, he saw a long, *long* neck, a drooping belly, and a tail curled like a whip.

He shifted his head to one side and took in the sight of the gigantic animals walking single-file ahead of him. He saw tails, enormous buttocks, legs like tree trunks, tubby bodies, long, lean necks, and at the end of them, camel-like heads bobbing to a rhythm only their owners could hear. Between the legs of the long-necks ran tiny, friendly-looking green-and-pink salamanders with beaks. They played happily, taking refuge from the rain under the bellies of the long-necks. It was so hot and humid that the rain barely cooled off anything.

Zane smelled something very bad. These guys were gas giants!

The weirdest thing of all was that he had played with toy long-necks when he was little. And the necks of *these* animals were wrong. They were held almost straight out, not up and curling into an *S*-shape as he'd expected. Their bodies were spotted. They were bumpy, lumpy, and wrinkled. They were gray and green and aqua. They were jiggly and wiggly. They were elephantine and blubberized.

He felt a whap against his backside. Another long-neck. The slap was meant to get his attention, nothing more. He'd stopped moving.

The thirteen-year-old in the body of the brontosaurus is holding up the amazing swaying conga line!

He walked with the herd along the curving shore. But he couldn't quite keep on course, like a Mack truck desperately in need of a wheel alignment—

Sploosh-splash-splish-splosh.

He was in the water, up to his ankles. The little green-and-pink dinosaurs returned to the shore, avoiding the splattering caused by his missteps. He watched as they stopped now and then to pick at algae or other plants washed ashore.

Cahhhrrr!

Zane walked onto the shore and looked up.

Whoa!

The ground fell away, and his noodle was suddenly a good thirty feet in the air. Winged creatures circled the skies. One came in for a landing on the back of another brontosaur. It had long reddish yellow wings and a thin beak half the length of its body. A pterodactyl! Neat!

He saw other pterodactyls land near the shore, sailing in like gulls. They went after enormous shells, pulling squids and other weird-looking, goopy, gelatinous, veiny things out of them to munch on. One stuck its long beak in the sand and burrowed until it came up with a worm the size of a snake. The pterodactyl swallowed it whole.

"That was disgusting," Zane muttered.

A dragonfly with a two-foot wingspan dive-bombed from his left. Zane wailed and drove his head into the water at his feet. It was like plunging off a diving board.

Whhhhhaaaaahhhhhh! Splash!

Under the water, weird little fish sailed by. One

looked like a fish-eater kind of fish with tiny, nasty teeth. And there was something like a baby shark advancing on it, followed by a shark that wasn't a baby. He saw something that looked like a *ray* or something. It was as long as the shark, and it had bright green fluttering wings, an arrow point on its tail, and great big nasty teeth—

Zane pulled his head from the water, nearly stumbling as he tried the difficult non-Arthur-Murray-approved brontosaurus sidestep. He settled back into his place in line, content not to think about anything except keeping *out* of the ocean.

It didn't last. He had started *thinking*. That was dangerous. There was no telling where it might lead.

Of course, he'd always known the answer to that when his father was still around.

What are you, a moron? A B-minus? You can do better than this. And this A? Just an A. I used to get A-pluses.

But his father was out of the picture now. Dear old Dad had his new family in Seattle, and every month he sent his check. *This is twice what the courts say I have to send. All I'm looking for in return is a little peace and quiet, a little privacy.*

In other words, no calls. No letters. No visits. No contact whatsoever.

We need that check, his mom would say. And Zane knew they did.

He watched the other dinosaurs and considered how slow-moving and aimless they seemed. He'd been to summer school once and recalled the faces of his bored, uninterested fellow students. It was awful, but at least it had prompted a letter from his father.

I'm very disappointed in you.

Zane had had to fight the temptation to have the letter framed.

A small figure trotted along at his right flank. A baby brontosaurus! It was *so* cute! Zane carefully lowered his long neck and got a better look.

"Hey, little guy."

The baby bronto had huge, fluttering lips. *That* was different. The little guy opened his mouth—and belched right in Zane's face!

Gahhhrrr-plllmmmph!

"Bleh!" Zane cried. "Thank you so much!"

The baby bronto trotted off, looking happy as all get out.

"Like I'm gonna let you get away with that," Zane said, sensing the possibility of some fun.

Zane broke from the herd and chased after the little dinosaur—and tripped—landing flat on his belly like a baseball player sliding into home base.

A shrill cry sounded from the little one. It ran toward a line of leafy trees. Other long-necks went over and started licking the baby with their wet tongues. Some stared, and Zane felt as if he was being examined by a pack of long-necked physicians. All they needed were white coats and stethoscopes.

This patient is a lame-o, his pratfall wasn't the least bit funny.

Zane stood up. "I'm all right. But, boy, is this a tough room..."

Zane tried more physical humor. But the long-necks didn't get it, so he gave up. A few of the long-necks were nibbling at the low vegetation near the trees. The little guy was with them.

"Hey, Runt!" Zane cried out in alarm. "You're eating rocks. What's *that* about? You're gonna have rocks in your head!"

Runt kept at it. Zane nibbled on some leaves. He looked over and saw a pair of long-necks rubbing up against each other. They were—necking.

Then a third long-neck appeared. He didn't look happy. A jealous boyfriend? Zane didn't know. He watched as the third long-neck curled his tail and—

Whhhhhppppphhhh-thhhhhhhhappppppppppp!!!

A crack like Indiana Jones's whip sounded in the air, and a terrifying vibration shuddered through him. It was like being slapped by Moe, Larry, and Curly with the super-speed of the Flash. The little green dinosaurs that had been running in and out between the legs of the long-necks now scattered for cover. The discouraged couple split up and went back to the shore.

Pretty soon, it was back to the conga line. Feeding time was over. Runt came trotting up beside Zane.

"Go away, kid. Ya bother me."

The mini-bronto didn't go. He leaped around, anxious for attention. Then he made a low, deep *whhhhhhrrrmmmm* sound.

"Go away!" Zane said, bumping the little guy with his backside. Runt flopped over, scrambled to his feet, and trotted away, making shrill bleating noises.

Oh, like he was really upset.

Zane had an idea of what was behind those cries. The runt just wanted attention.

A huge form approached. A long-neck that was even bigger than Zane.

"What's up, Stretch?" Zane asked.

Stretch nudged Zane with his neck.

"What?"

The nudge came again. Harder. This was weird. On one side, he could see the bigger dinosaur, and it looked like it was scowling at him. On the other side, he could see Runt running toward an opening between the trees.

"You want me to go after him?" Zane asked.

"Rhhhhrrr, rhhhhrrr!" the long-neck articulately replied.

"He's faking! I know all about faking! I do it on exams all the time. Maintaining a C-minus average isn't easy; you have to know the answers to make sure you're marking stuff wrong. Trust me, it's an act!"

Crrrrrrrrracckkkkkkk!

Zane jumped. More long-necks crowded around, whipping their tails. Two actually slapped him with their tails!

"Okay, okay! I'll bring him back!"

Zane took off. Like it or not, he would have to face the world...

CHAPTER 4

WILL

Will lay on the ground amidst a carpet of exhausted raptors. He had been thinking about Bertram's message and wondered what Lance would say. Actually, he *knew* what Lance would say.

This is your chance. Things don't get much more spectacular than this, do they? The whole future's riding on you! You got just what you wanted.

Will forced that thought away. True, the lightning had sought him out and struck him first, then flowed from his hands toward Patience and Zane. But he hadn't set all this into motion—he would never have wanted this.

Will sighed. He was starving again, and that made it hard to think about the big, cataclysmic event that was supposed to occur right here in a couple of days. He'd racked his brain trying to figure out what could possibly happen that he—or anyone else—could prevent.

And he'd come up with *nothing*. That had left him with one thing to think about:

HUNGRY-HUNGRY-HUNGRY-GIMME-HUNGRY

His appetite. Will had taken only one quick bite earlier in the day. The pack had devoured the rest.

The other raptors still seemed hungry, too. Even with the food supply gone, they trudged up the hill, and Big Guy displayed his prowess by fending them off.

It was a raptor thing, Will supposed...

He lay on his side, his stomach making gurgling noises. Closing his eyes against the glare of the sun, he thought about the contents of his refrigerator back home. Ripe fruit. Hot dogs. Homemade potato salad. Sandwich meats. Salad fixings. Cold sodas.

Then a voice came to him.

"Naw, I'm not hungry. I'll just grab something at school."

It was his voice. *He* had said those words. There had been a time in his life when he had shrugged and said he didn't feel

HUNGRY-HUNGRY-HUNGRY.

Will began to beat his head against the ground. And he wasn't the only one.

All the raptors were hungry and miserable. And still, Big Guy wasn't letting them search for food. One or two had tried, and other adult raptors had hauled them back.

A squeal and the sound of a raptor sliding down the hill brought everyone around. Will opened his eyes.

There were no contenders left on the mountain. Every raptor had been tested against Big Guy and found wanting. Every one except Junior, of course. Big Guy was strutting, his favorite pal strutting with him. Both came down from the hill like they were all that and a bag of—

No, no, no, don't say it, Will thought.

But there it was. *Chips.* Potato chips. And not the "lite" kind, either. Suddenly, he could smell a whole bag of greasy potato chips, and he could almost taste them, too. He held out his claws.

"CAN WE GET SOMETHING TO EAT NOW?" Will hollered with what felt like the last of his strength.

The others stared at him as if he just committed the most rude act imaginable—short of challenging Big Guy directly.

Even Binky was moving away from him.

He *hadn't* just challenged Big Guy, had he?

Big Guy and Junior came bounding over. Will wobbled to his feet. The mighty raptor peered down at him. The sun was behind Big Guy's head, so all Will could see of the raptor's face was a pair of angry eyes. Then Big Guy moved past him, bashing his shoulder into Will's. It spun him and set him up perfectly for Junior's attack.

The smaller raptor let out an ear-piercing series of yips. Will drew back, more startled than anything, and Junior passed him by without a second glance.

Didn't answer my question, Will thought. This time, he kept himself from saying anything aloud.

Then it came to him. He'd been looking at this all wrong. There was nothing in this valley but the raptors. If something big was going down, it would involve *them*. And if it involved them, Big Guy would be at the center of it.

So the best way Will could find out what was going on would be if he was up there *with* Junior, at Big Guy's side. He had to become part of the inner circle.

Finally, a challenge he could handle!

Now the other raptors were on their feet. Big Guy and Junior stood before the group like a pair of army officers. Big Guy would nod toward a certain raptor, and it would line up behind him. Then Junior would do the same.

Buddy was among the first chosen. Big Guy grabbed him.

Were they picking teams? It'd be kinda hard playing shirts and skins with *this* crew...

Then it came to him. Hunting parties! They were dividing up the raptors into two hunting parties.

That *had* to be it!

Soon, a dozen raptors stood behind each team

leader. Only...no one was picking *him*.

Finally, it came down to Will and Binky. They stood alone, unchosen. Will had seen this scenario played out countless times in gym class. He was often a team leader who'd grudgingly—while not trying to seem like there was any grudgingness—picked one of the remaining klutzy, dorky, *unworthy* candidates.

Now it was Big Guy who had to choose.

"Come on," Will said. "I'm fast, I'm smart, I can—"

Big Guy chose Binky.

Junior hollered and growled, but Big Guy smirked—if such a thing was possible for an ugly-faced raptor. Junior glared at Will and turned his back. Will looked at Big Guy, who nodded in Junior's direction.

Humiliation. He felt like a joke.

And from the looks he was receiving from all the other raptors, that pretty much summed up Will's new existence.

Well...he'd just have to work on that.

Big Guy led his raptors to the east while Junior and his pack headed west. Will looked back and saw that the raptors following Big Guy were pretty much behaving themselves. A few flashing claws, a kick here and there, some snapping teeth. But the group stayed together.

It was different with his party. Junior's group quickly spread apart as little cliques formed. Junior turned and yipped at the others, but after several miles the hunting party had dissolved into small bands that seemed to have little interest in the common good.

The foraging went badly. The land was dry, the hills without life. Will wondered why such a large group of predators had come to this place.

Then he smelled it. A scent that was sweet, luscious and delectable—

Hello, meat!

The scent *seemed* fresh. It was everywhere—and nowhere—all at once. Maddening! This had to be what had drawn so many raptors to one spot.

Will had sat through enough of Mr. London's lectures to understand at least a little of how things worked in the Mesozoic. He knew that certain animals followed migratory patterns, leaving the north when the cold began and hiking south.

It made sense that the raptor packs, ravenous as they were, could have been following some herd of what Mr. London had affectionately termed "veggiesaurs." And somewhere in this valley, the predators had lost them. But how was that possible?

Another mystery. Could this have something to do with—

Will spotted movement. He spun, swiveling his head so quickly that it nearly made him dizzy. One of the big, fat, juicy ratlike mammals raced through a tangled, skeletal maze of hard, dry brush.

"Yeah, yeah, yeah, *yeah!*" Will hollered. In his head, he heard the words. In his ears, his cries sounded more like yips. He pounced, raking at the brush, but his prey was crafty.

He heard the trampling footfalls of a half-dozen other raptors rushing in. They'd heard his yips. He growled and spat at them.

"Mine! Mine! Bug off!"

Like they cared. Will hated this. He vowed that if he ever got back to his own body, it would be veggies and nothing but veggies. But for now he was—

HUNGRY-HUNGRY-HUNGRY

—and he just couldn't help himself. He was a carnivore, a meat-eater, whether he liked it or not. And dinner was getting away!

Will chased the ratlike mammal. It scurried, zigzagged, and sped to higher ground. Will zipped past a pair of twisted trees that had been bent all the way back like bows. He skipped along rock ledges. He leaped and scrambled and crawled.

As he ran, he marveled at the power of this body. He felt like he was dirt-biking in the mountains back home!

Another strange scent came to him. A *nest* of the ratlike mammals! Will scanned the ground, searching for it.

In the shade of a huge, leaning stone, Will saw a mass of squirming bodies. How many were there? Dozens? Hundreds? Big Guy was gonna *love* him!

The other raptors were coming up fast. The pint-size mammals scattered, racing in every direction.

The raptors divided up. Will was alone again—or almost. One raptor was suddenly nipping at his heels.

Junior. The dried brush crunched beneath his feet. Junior extended his sickle claws—SNICK-SNICK— and tore at the brush with each step. Fleeing prey climbed higher—higher—up a big hill.

Some shred of human intellect still in Will now understood that there was a danger. But it was hard to listen to it. The yattering, chattering squeals of the prey rang in his ears.

The mammals were moving into the open where they could be grabbed. Will couldn't stop following the instinct to leap onto the hill's plateau where the meat would be exposed, vulnerable, unable to get away.

MEAT-MEAT-HUNGRY-HUNGRY-HUNGRY-HUNGRY

He was in the air, yipping with laughter. He screeched as he struck a stone with one clawed foot and *pinwheeled* with his little arms. He teetered back and forth on an incredible brink, one leg poised outward.

Junior grabbed Will's arm and steadied him. Will looked down at the sharp drop before them. A great ravine, and an unnatural one.

Earthquakes, Will thought. *Quakes created enormous cracks in the ground...*

Some of the mammals scurried down that sheer wall toward those cracks—to safety. But most of them didn't make it.

The other raptors raced toward them, capturing prey in their claws. Will's heart raced. Saliva dripped from his maw in anticipation. And—

Something struck his back. Hard. He was again tumbling end over end down the side of a hill. He landed hard and scrambled to his feet. He looked up to see the other raptors gathering at the hill's apex, anxious to impress Junior with the spoils they had collected.

That surprised Will. He thought the group had no loyalty to Junior, that it was Big Guy they feared.

The food was dropped to the ground. Feeding frenzy! This time, for *real!*

All the other raptors came running. Soon they were in a huddle, and disgusting chewing and *spitting* sounds filled the air.

Instinct told Will that this was wrong. He thought about the collection of food Big Guy had been guarding earlier in the day, and something just didn't track...But Will couldn't begin to understand the ways of these animals.

Soon the feast was over, and Will was the only

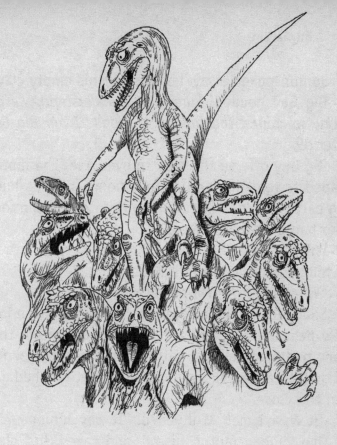

one without a full belly. The other raptors came down the hill, and Will slipped past them to see if any food had been left. Nothing remained.

With his stomach clutching and growling and howling, Will followed the pack toward the gathering place farther down the valley.

It was nearly an hour later when Big Guy and his division arrived. They were carrying their spoils. Big Guy had his hunters set the food in a vast collection, then looked over at his favorite.

Junior looked away, holding out his empty claws.

Big Guy nodded. *Sure, kid, I understand, we got lucky, we found the food, you didn't. I am Big Guy, after all.*

Big Guy offered the food to everyone. The raptors leaped toward the food—those from Big Guy's hunting party, who hadn't eaten, and those from Junior's, who had but wanted more.

Will ran with the others. Big Guy stepped in front of him, then roared in displeasure.

"What'd I do?" Will demanded.

Suddenly, he understood. Will smelled of the food he'd been near. Junior and all the members of their pack had made a wide path around Big Guy for fear of their treachery being discovered. But Will had gotten too close.

"It wasn't me!" Will yelled. "It was Junior—"

The bigger raptor hissed and raked his claws toward Will. Then he drop-kicked Will away and turned his back on him.

A half hour later, while Will sat alone and apart from the others, Buddy came over and dumped some food at Will's feet.

Will reminded himself that he was a human being, that this was temporary, and that he should conduct himself with some decorum and not just—

He pounced on the grub, kicking, snarling, and devouring it just like everyone else. From somewhere close, he heard a growl of displeasure. It definitely came from Big Guy.

Tearing and slobbering and eating with such abandon that he actually cried, Will ignored the leader. He'd get in good with Big Guy. But for now, he had to eat!

When Will was done, he looked up, anxious to thank Buddy. But his friend had gone, leaving him completely alone.

CHAPTER 5

ZANE

Zane was lost. No question about it. He had spent *hours* looking for Runt, stumbling through the pouring rain. It had been tough going. He had had to squeeze between trees. After a while, the spaces between the trees widened, and he had found ponds for drink and lots of vegetation to eat.

He'd seen ratlike things with grinding teeth and millions of little lizards and frogs—this world was alive with them. It was as if they fell from the skies along with the driving rain.

He knew he'd dream of them tonight—salamanders and frogs raining from the skies on a commando mission to tickle him senseless.

He made his way through forest and marsh and arrived at a broad stretch of green rolling hills. The sky was gloomy gray. Zane sensed he was getting close to his quarry, because he had figured out another way of tracking Runt.

With his nose.

He could smell the little brat. Runt had a distinctive odor, somewhere between a week-old fart and coconut cereal. *Why* coconut cereal, he didn't know, but there it was.

"When I get home, I am never having coconut cereal again," Zane groused.

The smell was getting stronger, and that was good—horrible as the smell was. It meant he was getting close.

If he could just find Runt, he was sure he could get back to the herd. Before night, he hoped.

All he had to do was ignore the pull from the direction of Will and the others. Easy, right?

Zane tromped up a hill and spotted his quarry. Runt stood on the crest of the next hill, chewing on some greens. He looked tiny in the distance, though Zane knew Runt was really the size of a VW Bug.

Well, everything's relative...

Suddenly, he *knew* why he had been chosen to go after the runaway bronto—and it didn't have anything to do with Zane's "scaring" the little guy.

Runt was his baby brother.

"No," Zane whispered. "Don't do this to me. *Please...*"

But it was true. Zane could sense their connection. It was as if the Psychic Friends Network was dialing him up and delivering the news personally.

Hello, Zane? This is your inner dinosaur checking

in. You wanted to know what your future holds?

Zane looked at the wide, jiggling backside of the young brontosaurus. "Say it ain't so."

Sorry, kiddo. Runt's your responsibility—perma-nently. Have a nice day, and try not to freak when you see the charges on your phone bill.

He couldn't believe it. He *wouldn't* believe it! He knew all about baby brothers. He'd been one to his four sisters. There was no way he was going to accept this sick twist of fate!

Zane walked until he reached the hill. Runt grunted and barely glanced at him.

Zane felt a tickling at his nose and a tingling at the back of his head. The feeling made his skull wobble and his neck muscles tense.

They weren't alone.

The other dinosaur stood at the bottom of the hill. It looked like a T. rex, but it had a wriggling sail down its back. The creature was a golden brown with forest-green and burgundy streaks. This was a *guy* dinosaur. Zane could sense it somehow...*predator.*

With a honk of fear, Runt raced down the far side of the hill!

Screaming in absolute terror, Zane followed Runt. The sailback roared and came after them.

It came up *fast.* The sailback arrived beside Zane's flank and opened its maw.

A flare of pain! Zane had been bitten!

Zane saw the meat-eater's maw open again.

"No!" he shouted. Zane's tail curled up just as the sailback was about to sink his claws into his flank—

CCRRRRRRACCKKKKKKKKKKKKKKKKKK!

The sound was like a thunderclap, an explosion. It was deafening and terrifying and—

The sailback ran away, quivering and shaking, and disappeared into the rain.

It took Zane a second to realize *he* had done that. He used his tail again.

CRRRACKKKKKKK!

Zane ran on, the cold rain in his face. Every step he took hurt. Moving was making his wound worse. But he couldn't stand still. The sailback could come back, it could—

It came back.

Zane saw it charging at him. It snapped and chomped at the empty air next to his body, retreating only when Zane whipped his tail and made a thunderclap.

Then the predator raced to his other flank, always avoiding the reach of his tail.

Zane felt himself slowing down. He was breathing hard. But the sailback looked tireless.

Zane felt every childhood terror he'd ever imagined embodied by the thing at his heels. He wished he was in his room, in his own bed, where he could pull the blankets over his head when there was something scary that he didn't want to face.

Suddenly, he heard a rustling from above and a loud, comforting *snap*. A huge baby blue form descended from the gray sky and settled on him, covering his head and half of his body.

His blanket!

No, that couldn't be!

But the weight that covered him was powder fresh. Soft and fuzzy. Warm and protective. And he couldn't see where he was going!

There really is a big blankie hanging over me! What the—?

The sailback roared. Zane shook his head free.

The predator was coming again.

Suddenly, a strong, terrible scent drifted down to him. It was the smell of burned barbecue, greasy oil, and his pet salamander, Fred, all at once.

At the crest of the hill stood a second sailback.

"No!" Zane whipped his tail.

CRRRRRRRRRRRRACCKKKKKKKKKKKKKKKKKKK!

The sailback behind him stopped. The one on the top of the hill flinched but held its ground. A small pink-and-green dinosaur stood beside the determined sailback on the hill

"The tail, yes, good!" the pink-and-green dino called. "The bones in the end of your tail are only six inches long. That's what gives you the incredible range and variety of motion. Used like a whip, your tail can travel at more than seven hundred miles an hour! Hit the Acrocanthosaurus with it!"

The salamander was talking. It was *talking!*

Or, rather, as the animal chittered, Zane heard human speech in his head.

"Let me handle this," said the sailback. *Patience!*

Patience roared—and the sailback behind Zane stopped in its tracks, tilting its head curiously.

"Back off, loser!" howled Patience.

The dinosaur raised its jaw majestically, nodded once, and turned away. Zane watched it thread its way back over the hill, and it was gone!

"Do you have a name?" Patience asked.

"It's—it's me," Zane said. "Crazy Zane!"

Patience looked down at the salamander. "He'll slow us down, and he's useless in a fight."

"He's hurt," the other said. "And he's one of us."

"Mr. London?"

"Call him Bob. It annoys him," Patience said.

"Yes," the little dinosaur said. "I'm Mr. London."

Zane was in no mood to annoy anyone. He was relieved to see others. "That thing was *after* me. I thought—"

"Can't we just clean him up, find a safe place for him to hide, and leave him?" Patience asked.

"There are no safe places," Mr. London said. "And it's a moot point. With Bertram and the others, they had to be together or else the machine wouldn't take them home."

Patience growled in frustration. "Just perfect..."

"Waitaminute," Zane said. "What are you talking about? I thought you *liked* me. What you did for me in the hall, the way you nailed that jerk—"

"Didn't mean a thing," Patience said.

"Okay...," Zane said in a low voice. He looked at Mr. London. "How did you know I was not another dinosaur?"

"We could hear you shouting," Patience said, spinning angrily in his direction. "And the *blankie* was a dead giveaway."

Zane shifted the blanket down his neck a little.

"Yeah," he said in surprise. "It's still here. How'd I do *that?* I was just thinking about it and—"

"I think I understand!" Mr. London said excitedly. "When the others came back, they were able to manifest certain psychic abilities. These abilities became more powerful when the students were placed under extreme stress."

"Psychic abilities?" Zane asked.

"Powers of the mind," Mr. London said. He rose on his hind legs and touched the blanket. "It's how we're able to hear each other in words above the grunts and roars and chirps our physical bodies are making. But this illusion is so complete. I can feel the blanket's texture, I can smell its newly washed freshness. This is amazing!"

"Okay," Patience said. "So maybe he won't be *totally* useless. Whenever there's danger, he can summon his magic blanket. I'm feeling safer already."

"Hey!" Zane said, swiveling his head around. "What's your problem? I never did anything to you!"

"You're *here,*" Patience said. "That's enough."

Zane felt a chill. The rain was pelting his hide again. What had happened?

"The blanket!" Mr. London said. "It vanished!"

Zane looked over his shoulder. The blanket was gone.

Mr. London nodded. "When you were distracted, the illusion faded. So concentration is a factor. I can see many uses for this power. And considering your imagination—yes, yes indeed!"

Zane couldn't believe this. A teacher was praising him. Boy, his dad would *love* that.

Patience bore down on Zane.

"Focus," she said. "We're going to Ground Zero. Where it's going to be *dangerous*. I want to hear that you're committed to this. Because I don't want to be here. I didn't ask for *any* of this. All my life, other people have been deciding where I'm going to live, shoving me from one foster home to another, to places that are—"

She shivered slightly. "The Mushnicks, the people I'm living with right now? Stan and Judy tell me that I'm lucky because I know what my life's worth. Six hundred and ninety-five dollars a month."

She paused. "That's how much the state pays them to take care of me. It's what they make for letting me have a room and a key to that dump they call a home..."

"That's what you want to get back to?" Zane asked quietly.

"*Yes,*" Patience spat. "Mushnick's First Law. Keep your head down and just get through. I'm lousy at the first part. The second part—getting through—is what keeps me going."

She looked at the brontosaurus.

"I'm going back so I can finish my time, then go

where I want and do what I want. So I'm telling you again, we're going to Ground Zero. And I'm asking you, can you stick it out with the rest of us?"

No, heck no, not a chance, Zane thought. But what was the alternative? It was just like in school. He needed to be protected. And he hated it.

"I'm in," Zane said. He climbed to the top of the hill and saw Runt approaching from the other side. A noise came out of the baby brontosaurus. A tiny coo that sounded just enough like a roar to make it clear that he was trying to imitate Patience.

Wait! I can't just abandon Runt.

Which really sucked.

"Excuse me," Zane said to Patience. "There's just one other thing..."

CHAPTER 6

WILL

Will felt desperate as he wandered through the raptor pack, trying to come up with a plan. He had his goal in sight. Every time he looked at Junior smugly standing at Big Guy's side, he thought, *I need to be where you are, pal. Whatever's gonna happen, Big Guy will be at the center of it. So I've got to be in good with him.*

But Big Guy couldn't stand Will. He'd humiliated the larger raptor by getting past him and spilling the food out of the cave. And then there had been the "incident" with the food gathering...

Buddy had been protecting Will by keeping him out of Big Guy's path and calming Junior whenever *he* came around looking for a fight. Buddy was resting now, lazing in the sun. And while he appreciated Buddy's efforts, Will knew he couldn't avoid the pack leader forever. He had to find a way to turn things around!

He walked right up to Big Guy.

"Hey! Lookin' good, lookin' sharp. I see some of those teeth are growing back. That's great!"

Will was knocked down the side of yet another hill.

They don't like when I talk. It wigs them out. I keep forgetting.

Will's actions would have to speak for him.

He heard grunts and a couple of *SNICK-CLICKS*. Near a sheer mountain wall, a pair of raptors were fighting. Big Guy didn't like it when the pack fought among themselves. Will scanned the valley and spotted Big Guy.

Junior lay napping nearby.

Perfect.

Will leaped to the center of the ring of raptors that circled the combatants. The fighters might have been twins. Each had lobster-colored scales and little green dots scattered across its body like measles.

Big Guy usually settled arguments with a few roars and a couple of well-placed swipes. But Will wasn't Big Guy. He was feeling more comfortable in his raptor body, but not enough to jump between duelists armed with sickle claws. He was certain, however, that if he could get these two to settle down, he would impress Big Guy.

A couple of raptors gave him strange looks and stepped away. Their reaction sparked an idea in Will.

"A vote for me is a vote for all of us," he said

boldly. "Go with what you know!"

The raptors yipped, and a few moved away.

What was it Briefcase Man had said? *You have a negative, turn it into a positive. That's how you get ahead in this world!*

Will focused on the fighters and took a deep breath before he yelled, "Yo! Pea Brain! Stupid!"

The combatants stopped and stared.

Good. He had their attention. Now he had to make them see the error of their ways, that was all.

"I bet you guys are really good friends," Will said.

The raptors were glaring at Will.

"Whatever you're fighting about, it's really no big thing. It never *is*. I'm sure you can just work it out."

What was he talking about? Pea Brain and Stupid were advancing on him.

"Whoa, back off, guys. I'm trying to be the voice of reason."

Will banged into another raptor, who kicked him in the rump, and he went sprawling. A chorus of yips erupted.

Laughter. Great.

Will felt like an idiot. Then he thought about it. At least they were loosening up.

A green-and-yellow-scaled raptor struck at the back of another. It was probably a harmless gesture. *Hey, look at that, isn't that funny?*

But the other raptor didn't take it that way. He

snarled and kicked, driving the off-balance raptor into two others—who didn't take the invasion of their personal space all that kindly, either.

Will saw Big Guy heading their way. This was not going the way he had planned.

"Guys, you gotta chill! Come on!"

He had forgotten about Pea Brain and Stupid. They knocked him down and kicked him savagely. The more he yelled, the harder they struck.

"Binky! Buddy! Help me!"

Suddenly, Pea Brain yelped in surprise and was pulled back. There was a grunt, and Stupid was flung aside. Will looked up to see the face of his savior.

Big Guy stared down at him, Junior at his side.

Dazed, Will looked at the chaos. Where there had been two battling, there were now dozens. Big Guy hissed at Will but had no time to punish him. Will knew *that* would come later.

Why can't you guys be more like sharks? Will wondered. He had once read that sharks had limited memories. If something happened to a shark, fifteen minutes later it was completely forgotten.

But Will had already learned that raptors weren't like that. Now he had messed up in front of Big Guy. *Again.*

Suddenly, his body trembled. A shuddering wave of force reached up from the soles of his feet and gripped him. His world rumbled and shook.

A pebble struck him from above. Will looked up and saw the sheer cliff face rippling and cracking. Stones fell. One the size of his head struck the ground at his feet with the impact of a bomb.

"Rock slide!" Will yelled.

The raptors weren't listening. They just kept fighting. The world could have been ending around them and they wouldn't have paid attention!

Will didn't know what to do.

The sheer cliff face continued to split and shudder. The ground writhed. Raptors were tossed from their feet, and the skirmishes finally ended. Pebbles and rocks dropped like fiery comets in the bright sunlight.

One struck Will's shoulder and spun him around. He heard a grunt as another raptor hurtled backward, a boulder caught in his arms.

We're at Ground Zero, Will thought wildly. But there were supposed to be two more days!

The raptors raced in every direction. Some flung themselves into the path of the falling stones. Others narrowly avoided disaster. A spiderweb of cracks sketched itself across the face of the cliff.

An entire sheet of stone thirty feet across slid toward Big Guy, whose back was turned.

Junior wasn't around. Only Will was close enough to save Big Guy. This was his chance!

He ran toward Big Guy as a great shadow

descended upon him. He leaped, feet first, and
kicked Big Guy, who yipped in surprise.

Both Will and Big Guy hit the ground rolling as
the stone sheet fell to the earth where they had been
only a second before.

Bits of stone cut them. Big Guy shielded his face,
but Will could not keep himself from watching the
stone land with a deafening crash.

Now the ground was settling. It was over. Will looked at Big Guy and saw *Junior* next to him. Junior helped the raptor rise and was patted on the arm for his trouble.

"Hey, waitaminute," Will said. "He wasn't around. It was me! I—"

Big Guy growled and kicked a rock at Will. It sailed past his head. Junior appeared to smirk as he went off with the pack leader.

I do the work, you take the credit.

Will surveyed the earthquake's aftermath. There were raptors half-buried under stone. Some were hurt. Big Guy began to dig for one. Will eagerly rushed to Big Guy's side to help, but the leader growled and bit the air.

He blames me for all of it, Will thought bitterly. *The big brawl. The ones who were hurt...*

"I was just trying to help," Will said. But he knew that he'd only been trying to help *himself*.

CHAPTER 7

PATIENCE

Patience trudged on.

The rain fell, and the landscape was a long series of rising rust-colored hills and ever-widening rock-strewn or muddy valleys. There was plenty of vegetation. Patches of trees and bushes, greens that were nice and soggy and covered in bugs. Yum. *If* you were a plant-eater like the lumbering pain-in-the-neck who'd stopped to graze behind her. She could hear him talking to his new baby brother.

"One can't forget to eat one's grinding stones, no, one cannot. And if one does, Mr. London is here to remind one."

"I heard that!" Mr. London called. He was scurrying ahead, generally avoiding the others.

"Look!" he cried. "More *Prisca reynoldsii* and *Pseudofrenelopsis parceramosa.*"

The Hypsilophodon attacked the funky flowering plants. They were few and far between in this era. Zane and Runt joined in the nibbling.

Patience had heard Mr. London catalog these plants before. The first, belonging to a family called *magnolids,* looked like puffy, bubbled-up, green-and-yellow Popsicles set on green stalks.

"These are like licorice sticks compared to most of the stuff back here!" Zane gobbled happily.

The other plants had dozens of serrated protrusions of bright red and soft, rich blue. They were a little tougher, more like Cracker Jacks on the outside with a little burst of pineapple flavor within, or so Zane reported.

"Stop that!" Mr. London suddenly hollered. "Stop! Stop!"

Patience was treated to the sight of Runt leapfrogging over her teacher as the rain poured down.

"Come on, Runt," Zane called. He rubbed his little brother's flank with his neck.

"Don't do that!" Mr. London hollered. "He might fall and squish me!"

"Squish *is* the technical term," Patience commented. "Heard it in class."

She watched as Zane tried to lure Runt away. Nothing worked. Zane shook his head, and his long neck moved with it like a golf putter.

"I wonder what I'd be doing if we were home. Probably staring at the bell, waiting for it to ring."

"Probably," Patience said.

"I miss that bell. I can just hear it—"

And, suddenly, so could they all. The bell rang, and Runt quickly abandoned Mr. London to race back to Zane's side, looking up expectantly. He seemed happy and excited.

"It's a game to him," Patience said. "He's so cute."

"Yeah."

"Can I eat him?"

"I wish." Zane sighed. "I don't think this body I'm in would appreciate it."

They were stuck with Runt, it seemed. He followed them everywhere and showed respect for Patience's status as a predator, but had little fear. In some ways, he was one of the boldest spirits she'd ever encountered. In other ways, the biggest pain. He almost made Zane seem tolerable.

Runt's attention seemed to be wandering. Zane made the bell ring again.

Brrrr-ring-ring-ring-ring-ring

Runt danced around, then nuzzled Zane's front right limb with his snout.

My hero...

Zane led Runt up the hill by making the sound of a telephone ringing while Patience and Mr. London followed fifty feet behind. Zane kept the little guy occupied with eggbeaters, wind chimes, and a couple of riffs from Santana as they walked on.

"'Can I *eat* him?'" Mr. London finally said to Patience. "Really. You seem to be in an even surlier mood than usual. I didn't think that was possible, but—"

Patience kicked at the Hypsilophodon. He raced out of her way. He was a fast little lizard.

"So what's eating you?" he asked.

"Stuff," she said.

"Ah. That's the extent to which you're willing to share? There's—stuff?"

"Yes." Patience looked away. She had felt unsettled ever since she'd had encountered the Acro attempting to eat Zane. The dinosaur had looked at her as if it knew her, and it had left the prey to her without a fight, in a gallant, gentlemanly way. She had felt a connection she couldn't explain to the green-and-golden-brown Acro.

She hadn't felt anything of the kind when she had fought Number 47. But this dinosaur, the Green Knight—he had some kind of history with her host. That both alarmed and intrigued Patience.

She looked at Zane's flank. She'd cleaned his wounds with fresh water. Then she'd used leaves coated with resin to clean the cuts. They'd served as bandages when they'd dried in place. Now the leaves were peeling off.

"How are you feeling?" she asked.

Zane tensed. He'd been worried about getting sick ever since Mr. London had happily shared a short biology lesson with them earlier.

"You see, when an Acrocanthosaurus fought a sauropod like yourself, the predator wouldn't expend useless energy or take undue risks. A few good bites like this, and the bacteria from the Acrocanthosaurus's mouth would provoke an infection.

"Then it was a matter of following the sauropod until it became sick. At length, it would collapse, unable to run any farther. The hunter would descend on its defenseless prey or signal other members of its tribe to come enjoy the feast."

A real motivational speech. Patience had the feeling Zane was thinking about Mr. London's words again.

"Um—how do I look?" he asked fearfully.

She just couldn't resist. "Actually," Patience began, "you *are* looking a little green."

Zane froze, then looked down at his scales. "Oh. Hah-hah. Big funny. And I thought I was the one who made the jokes around here."

"What use are you otherwise?" Patience said. He looked away.

Mr. London ran up between them. "We have a task we should be concentrating on. Bertram mentioned an amber key that we must find. Admittedly, it sounds like something from a PlayStation adventure, but—"

Zane's head swung around. "Will loves those games! We play 'em, and he's always saying the stakes aren't high enough, and he gets ideas to make the game better, and—"

"And the lightning came from *him*," Patience noted. "From his hands."

Zane stopped. "I'm not saying this is Will's fault or anything, that the machine picked up on his thoughts or something. No way. That's crazy."

"The machine responds to deep-rooted needs," Mr. London said.

"You should know," Patience said. "You set it off."

The teacher shuddered. "It doesn't matter who's to blame. We have to deal with the situation. Amber from the Triassic era has been found in Utah. The geologic record of Texas, however, is incomplete because sediment was moved by the influx and withdrawal of the inland sea. It's possible—"

"Conifer trees!" Zane said. "That's what we want. They make the resin that fossilizes into amber."

Patience narrowed her eyes.

Zane looked embarrassed. "My mom's an arborist. She tends trees. And—shop talk. I hear things."

"Oh," Patience said, masking her surprise.

"If it's fossilized, then it would have been buried by sediment and left undisturbed for millions of years," Zane said. "So—we can't be expected to start digging and exploring caves. Bertram would have told us. It's *got* to be in plain view, maybe so plain we'd stumble over it unless we thought to look."

Runt began stalking Mr. London.

Zane whipped his tail.

Thhhhhhwaccckkkkkkk!

The teacher ran. Patience shuddered and had to fight her own instinct to bolt. Runt raised his head defiantly and walked in the other direction.

Nothing scares this little guy, Patience thought. *Not even me. Too bad Zane didn't get any of that in <u>his</u> dinosaur.* Mr. London returned, still shaking.

"Let me try something," Zane said. He sank back on his haunches—and the upper half of his body rose high into the air. His neck craned up, his front legs kicked against empty air. His full weight suddenly rested on his back legs and tail, creating a tripod.

"I see some fissures to the west," Zane said.

"Seismic activity!" Mr. London said. "Earthquakes creating cracks in the earth's surface. That might reveal deposits of amber. Good thinking!"

"Yeah." Patience had to admit it *was* good thinking. So how could it have come from Zane?

The brontosaurus trembled in midair. "How do I get down?"

"Try to force your shoulders to relax," Mr. London said. "Come down gently, drop to all fours again, like a cat."

Zane tottered, and his tail caught between his legs and tripped him.

"AHHHHHHH!" he cried as he fell over on his side, the enormous bulk of his body—but not yet his head—slamming hard enough to send shock waves through the ground. Runt and Mr. London were bounced from the hillside by the impact.

Patience fell over, too. She and the little brontosaurus skidded to the base of the hill as Zane's head finally whiplashed into the dirt.

"Ow!" he wailed. "I cracked some teeth that time."

Zane wasn't able to figure out how to get up. Runt mimicked him and showed him the way.

"So," Patience said, "we head west."

As they walked, Zane began to chatter about comedians and old TV shows. Patience made it clear that she didn't watch a lot of TV—but that wasn't entirely true. In the middle of the night, when the Mushnicks were asleep, she would sneak out and play the tapes Holiday sent her. Vintage Michael Jordan. Kareem Abdul-Jabbar. Rodman. Even Shaq.

She'd met Holiday the past summer, after her seventh-grade friend Marcus had been hurt. Patience and Marcus had been on the track team together, and they loved to run. One day, Marcus had taken up a pole vault, cleared the beam, and landed a foot short of the pad.

He was never going to run again, and for Patience, returning to track and being reminded anew every day of what she had lost wasn't an option.

Holiday and his buddies had just graduated from high school, but they still played on Wetherford

High's grounds. She'd met them shooting hoops. Holiday was laughing at his friends.

"See that gangly girl? She can take you. She can take any of you!" he had said.

It had been a challenge. Patience had never been into hoops. But she *never* backed away from a challenge.

The first guy got the ball away from her but didn't keep it. "Someone tell Slick that basketball is *not* a contact sport!"

"It is the way *she* plays it," Holiday said. He introduced himself, saying he was called Holiday because with him, that's what every day was!

It was a good summer, over far too quickly. Holiday, whose real name was Kris, had enlisted in the army. But even after he'd begun his service, he sent her tapes to study.

"You get what you put into it," Holiday said. "I'm doing this to get my college money. But if you start now, those colleges will be lining up to give you scholarships. And that's a way out."

Patience's memory faded as the small group came to a collection of hills torn by fissures. They split up and looked around. Runt followed Mr. London.

"Not a lot of trees," Patience said.

"Twenty million years ago, this could have been a forest," Mr. London said. "One day, this will all be under water. Everything changes, given time."

Patience wondered if that could be true. As she looked into one fissure after another, she thought about Zane's weird behavior earlier.

She'd been impressed by his clear thinking but confused by his embarrassment about coming up with a good idea. And she knew for a fact that his mother wasn't a tree surgeon. Zane's mom was a secretary, studying to become a paralegal.

The Mushnicks complained when Zane's mother came to their store, because she never bought anything. She'd just look at the pretty jewelry, then move on.

Patience couldn't understand why Zane would lie about something like that, but she couldn't think of a reason to call him on it, either.

"I see something!" Mr. London yelled.

Patience followed Zane and Runt to the edge of a deep fissure.

"There," Mr. London said. "On the other side. About ten feet down."

Patience saw it. A hole that looked like it had been punched by a giant's hand. Within lay a small patch of amber.

A twenty-foot gap separated one edge of the fissure from the other. The crevice stretched across several hundred feet, then widened at either end of the horizon.

Zane lifted his head. "There's a land bridge a few

miles away, but I don't know how safe it is."

"Too far," Mr. London said. "It will be dark soon."

"Well, I could give you a ride on the Hoover express," Zane said. He walked up to the edge of the abyss, leaning his head out into the open air. His face reached almost to the hole bearing the amber.

"Yeah, it *looks* like a key."

He stepped back, pulling his head back over solid land again. "That was fun."

"All right, let's do it," Mr. London said.

Patience looked down over the edge. "That's a fifty-foot drop! What are we talking about, climbing on his head and—"

"Do you want to be stuck here all night?" Mr. London asked.

Patience thought about it. "No way."

"Then find some vine and let's get started."

Patience hated being ordered around. But she was too excited about getting home to say anything.

Soon, Mr. London was on top of Zane's head. The brontosaurus ushered him over the abyss.

"I'm feelin' a little woozy," Zane said suddenly.

"Don't!" Mr. London commanded.

"Ooh, I don't know..." Zane's head tipped from one side to the other.

"Stop that!"

"I can't help it. I'm a sickie."

Patience sniffed Zane's wound. There was no sign

of infection. Naturally, he was faking.

"Whoa!" Zane's head bobbed up and down. Mr. London held on, totally freaked.

I should say something, Patience thought. *I really should.*

"Just playing with you, Mr. L!" Zane said. "You've gotta—hey, dirt and dust, I—I—"

Chooooo-BLMMMMMPH!!!

Zane sneezed! A splatter of icky green mucus slapped against the wall before him. He shuddered and spilled Mr. London into the abyss.

The Hypsilophodon squealed as he dropped five feet. Then the safety vine caught him. He dangled under Zane's head, swinging from side to side like a pendulum. Zane sheepishly lifted his head out of the chasm and backed up. Patience fixed the quietly fuming Mr. London on his head again.

"Believe it or not, that was strangely exhilarating," Mr. London said. "I used to read adventure stories. I loved them so. Now—"

"Take two," Patience said.

The teacher nodded, and the descent was made quickly. Patience caught only a glimpse of a golden crystal streak in the shattered face of the wall below. She heard thumps behind her and turned to see Runt charging Zane's flank.

He thinks it's a game—he's going to ram Zane!

She opened her mouth to roar a warning.

"I've got it!" Mr. London yelled from below.

Patience didn't make a sound. She knew how easily Zane could be startled and didn't want to risk making him jump. If Mr. London fell again, he could drop the amber key.

Patience ran ahead and got between Runt and his target. He drew up short, looked away as if he hadn't been planning anything, and trotted off.

Patience looked at Zane's side and saw that the bronto was trembling. She sensed that he wasn't sick, He was nervous.

"Okay, up we go," Zane said jovially. "Nice and smooth. Yep. No problems here. Um..."

"Zane?" Patience said. "Is something wrong?"

"I ever mention I have a fear of heights?" Zane said.

You have a fear of everything, Patience thought. But she kept her mouth shut.

"This is no time for playing," Mr. London warned.

Patience saw Mr. London clutching a jagged amber spike with a crescent at one end. It really did look like a key.

Zane's head was bobbing and weaving.

"Close your eyes," Patience snapped.

"Oh, man," Zane whimpered.

"Do it!"

He did. She put her shoulder against his side and started pushing. "Back up!"

His big round belly quavered. "I—I—"

Zane sounded like he was going to pass out. Patience did the only thing she could think to do. She kicked him.

"Ow!" he said, bringing his head up sharply.

"Wahhh!" Mr. London yelled, holding on.

"Come on, keep it moving."

"Ughhh," Zane muttered. Soon his head was over solid ground.

Patience stomped over and bit through the line attaching Mr. London to the brontosaurus and hauled the teacher to safety. Zane dropped onto his side.

The impact shook the ground and toppled Patience. Rubble fell into the steep canyon. Zane moaned.

Patience got to her feet. Mr. London gave the closest he could to a thumbs-up. The key was safe. Patience walked around Zane's enormous body, stepped over his tail, and trod the length of him to stand next to his head.

"A while ago you went up into the air to impress me with how far you could see," she said. "You didn't get sick then. You wanna explain that?"

"Sight gag," Zane moaned. "Suffer. Art. Y'know. Had solid ground underneath. Owww. Neck sore."

His eyes fluttered open. "I got the key, though. Shows I'm not totally useless."

She had to admit that was true. "*Almost* totally

useless, but not totally useless."

Runt was near the edge, his neck hanging over the abyss. He made choking, whiny noises, then flopped back onto his side, imitating Zane.

The sky was turning black. A few stars had already appeared, shimmering through the drizzle.

Mr. London made the long trek around Zane's body and held out the key to Patience. "Touch it."

"What for?"

"I can't describe it. You should see for yourself."

Patience took the key. At first she felt nothing. It was small and brittle. She wondered if it was the actual key at all. Then she was overwhelmed by a sensation unlike anything she'd ever experienced.

Comforting. Warm. An electrical charge surged through her.

"It feels like *home,*" Mr. London said, his voice filled with wonder.

Patience *dropped the key*. Mr. London caught it before it struck the ground.

"What were you thinking!" he cried.

"*You* carry it," she shot back

"Certainly, I will!"

She looked up at the stars. That wasn't what home felt like to her. Except sometimes...in her dreams.

CHAPTER 8

WILL

Night had come. Will Reilly sat on a hill overlooking the valley of the raptors. A dim light shone down from the moon and stars, revealing the writhing bodies of the raptors as they danced. They were celebrating the day, the food they had gathered, and the pack's narrow escape from disaster.

Big Guy didn't dance, he brooded—never once looking up at the festivities. Junior kept everyone spellbound with his actions. Will envied him. He'd never been to a party where he'd sat outside, wishing he could be with the others. He'd always been the center of attention. He wondered if Junior was just popular—or one of the *elite*.

Will felt tired, alone, and scared. He was out of ideas, and in two days he'd be out of time. His head throbbed, his body ached, and he was cold. So *very* cold. He knew he wouldn't feel the chill if he could be down there dancing and enjoying himself.

But he also knew he wasn't welcome.

He closed his eyes and tried to make contact with the others. He reached out to them, anxious to hear their thoughts, to feel what they were feeling. He wanted to know if they were all right and were coming to help him.

Nothing.

He opened his eyes and looked down at the dancing, howling raptor pack. They were all having fun. Every one of them belonged. They were family. He had no one. If only Lance was around. Or Percy.

Even *Zane.*

No, *especially* Zane. Will was certain that if he could laugh, things might not seem so bleak.

He stood and stretched. He'd never had a plan fail like this before. Not that he'd always gotten what he wanted, but he'd learned if he set his sights high enough, he'd always achieve something worthwhile. His ultimate goal might remain out of reach, but he'd have some other prize to show for his efforts.

In school, for example, he'd tried to become the highest academic achiever, he'd worked hard to claim the top title. Instead, he'd come in third. But no one else could claim that distinction, and he was still up there with the others.

Not this time. He'd wanted to be *in* with Big Guy, one of the Knights of the Round Table. Instead, he wasn't even allowed to walk through the castle gates.

Will shivered. It was *so* cold! He thought of vacations he'd taken with his parents. Sitting before roaring fires, roasting nuts, telling stories...

For an instant, he could do more than imagine the comfort and warmth of a simple fire. His nostrils flared as he smelled its familiar scent. His mouth opened to take in the taste of the fiery, flickering heat. And his body was warmed.

A sharp *yip* sliced through the night.

Will looked down to see Junior knock another raptor down. Big Guy lifted his head and hissed. Junior scrambled away and went back to dancing.

Will shivered. He was still cold.

Well, Mister Academic Achiever, if you're so cold, do something about it!

Will knew that voice. It belonged to Briefcase Man. His dad. And the man wasn't being cruel. He was *right*.

"Things don't change unless you make them change," Will said out loud. A few of Briefcase Man's secret words of power.

He looked around. There was plenty of kindling. And this spot he had chosen would be a good one for a campfire. There were stones he could use to ring in the flames, but what could he use to make a spark?

Everything you need is right in front of you. You just need to sniff it out, Briefcase Man whispered.

He had to rely on his senses. His new senses.

Will drew in a full breath of thin mountain air. The stinky leathery luggage smell of the raptors filled him, along with a trace of the delectable scent that had brought the dinosaurs here.

There was more, and he needed to process everything.

Will breathed in again. This time he ignored the primary scents and tried to concentrate on all that was around him.

Limestone. The mountains were made of limestone!

Will hunted around in the dark until he came to one of the little tunnels used by the mammals. He dug and clawed until he had dislodged a few pieces of the deeper rock. He could use it like flint to make a fire!

"Scouts rule!" he said.

As the raptors danced below, Will gathered kindling and moved stones into place. Then he took the rocks he'd found and struck them together.

His first dozen attempts were failures.

"Some Boy Scout you are," Will muttered. But he knew that he'd been a *great* scout.

Keep at it, Briefcase Man whispered. *You know it can work.*

Will struck the stones together—and yelped with glee when he saw a spark!

It took a dozen attempts before he managed to

ignite a single branch, which sputtered and died. A dozen more, and a bigger branch ignited. Will stepped back and watched the blaze grow. He felt its heat. Basked in the glory of its light.

"I made this," he said proudly.

He wondered if he could find some nuts, or if there was a way to make popcorn.

Prehistoric popcorn. That'd be too wild!

Will approached the flames, though his inner dino warned him against it.

FIRE BAD-FIRE BAD-BURN STING

Will sat before the campfire, feeling happy and unafraid for the first time that night. This fire was such a simple thing, but it had every video game, movie, party—even every election—totally beat.

For a few wonderful moments, nothing else mattered.

Then he heard it. Silence. The yips had died away. The scuffling from the raptor dance had stopped and was replaced by stealthy footsteps and fearful honks.

"Oh, no," Will said.

The pack was coming.

Big Guy was the first to arrive. He looked grim. Other raptors leaped about, in excitement or perhaps in fear. Many stayed far back. Some gathered in little groups. A few squealed. Others chattered.

Will saw tails flickering and heard sickle claws extending.

CLICK-TAP-CLICK-TAP

He considered throwing dirt on the campfire. But it was too late. The raptors had him surrounded and would do whatever Big Guy wanted them to do.

Will heard a familiar yipping behind him. He didn't have to turn to know it was Junior. The young raptor was cackling—or so it seemed.

Big Guy took a step toward the blaze. Will didn't know what to do. There was nowhere to run. He'd fight if he had to, but he was inexperienced with this body. He didn't think he'd last very long before being overwhelmed by the others.

He watched as Big Guy stared down at the flames. A heavy branch fell and sparks flew up, accompanied by a sound like tin foil being crunched. Big Guy yipped. He appeared mesmerized by the flames. He sat before the fire, basking in its warmth.

Will saw the flickering orange glow on the big raptor's face begin to fade. Without thinking, he picked up a stick and stoked the fire. The flames leaped. Big Guy *cooed*. He looked from the fire to Will, and to the stick in Will's palm. Claws seized Will, and he was dragged down to sit next to the leader.

There was a breathy hiss, and Junior walked around to the other side of his father and kicked at the stones circling the flame. He got too close, and the fire singed his toes!

"Yiiiiieeee!" Junior wailed, hopping back on one foot. He spat in anger and frustration.

Big Guy ignored him. Other raptors took their places. Buddy sat beside Will. A raptor Will called the Ice Queen sat across from him.

Soon, all the raptors were gathered around the fire. Little fights broke out, and a few danced, but the warmth was lulling the raptors to sleep. Will kept the fire alive for several hours while Big Guy curled up beside it. The other raptors did the same. When Will tried to rise to get more wood, Big Guy hauled him down. Will stayed put.

Did I win over Big Guy? Will wondered as he drifted off to sleep. Once he'd stopped trying so hard, it had become a lot easier.

More words from Briefcase Man echoed in his mind as sleep overtook him. *Sometimes you have to slow down to go faster.*

Will hadn't understood that one until tonight. By moving slowly, by not desperately racing toward his goal—and stumbling and falling along the way—he'd achieved what he'd set out to do. Maybe Briefcase Man was smarter than he looked...

It was Will's last thought before drifting off.

Some time later, a sound woke him. A hiss that sounded next to his ear.

Will turned in surprise as a half dozen raptors launched themselves at him. He was so startled that he had no time to let out a howl of anguish. He was clawed and kicked and pummeled until he was too confused and dazed to fight back.

After the steady rain of blows had stopped, Will felt his body being dragged away. Big Guy lay undisturbed next to the orange embers of the dying fire, along with many other members of the pack. Will was hauled down into the valley, across a stretch of flatland, then up an all-too-familiar hill.

His attackers had been surprisingly quiet and self-controlled. Will had been dragged halfway up the hill on which Big Guy had tested the younger raptors when he came around long enough for that thought to occur.

Then he was pummeled again.

Finally, he felt himself being lifted, and he caught a glimpse of a single face in the moonlight.

"Junior?" Will moaned. His only answer was a hiss. Laughter? Contempt?

Suddenly, he was thrust into a dark, narrow space. His head struck solid rock, and he knew exactly what was going on.

Will was being stuffed into the narrow passage he had tried desperately to climb into earlier that day!

He fought, but Junior gripped his legs and pushed Will with all his strength.

No, Will thought. *This can't happen, it can't—*

"Ow!" he cried as his skull hit a rock. He tried to

unsheathe his claws but was too dazed. All he could do was throw a few little kicks at Junior.

The raptor spat in response—and pushed harder. Will's head struck more rock. A blinding light shone behind his eyes, coupled with intense pain. He heard rock falling around him, felt Junior pushing him toward—

What? He smelled fresh air once more. And something else. Then he was slipping down a long, winding tunnel, a narrow slide that sent him speeding ever downward. He crashed into another wall of earth and came to a painful, thudding halt. Rocks and soil buried him. Will felt their weight pressing on his strong but fragile body.

He smelled something—stronger than ever before. A ripe, pungent scent, rich and juicy. The scent that filled the entire valley!

HUNGRY-HUNGRY-HUNGRY

He dug frantically, his human brain lost to the fear and primal desires of his inner dinosaur. One thing human remained. Anger drove him on.

He'd done it! He'd finally achieved what he set out to achieve, and Junior had—

Suddenly, the dirt and rock gave way, and he was sliding again! He sped deeper into the hole, hearing rocks falling on the shelf on which he'd landed, closing the hole once more. He spun toward a sharp turn and whacked his head on the rock—and came to a stop. He was dangling over *nothingness*—a black void. A low rumble came from something ahead.

Will whipped his tail, kicked his legs, and was propelled forward. He dropped ten feet and struck solid ground. The impact was jarring! He moaned and cradled his right arm. His leg felt twisted.

Oh, man, what had they done to him? Where was this place and—

HUNGRY-HUNGRY-HUNGRY

—what was that smell? Will's vision began to clear. Glowing patches of phosphorescence clung to the ceiling of a huge cave. He was barely able to make out something big moving in the darkness. Another dinosaur! This one was three times his height. Vast and meaty, it gave off the scent he and the other raptors had been drawn to earlier.

LEAP-REND-TEAR-EAT IT-EAT IT-EAT IT

His instincts didn't care that this thing was alive. Or that it was enormous. Or about anything except

HUNGRY-HUNGRY-HUNGRY

But Will cared. He was alone and in no shape to take on a dinosaur this big.

"I'm not gonna hurt you," Will said.

The figure in the darkness stopped. It snuffled.

"I promise. I don't think I could if I wanted to. And I really don't want to."

A low cry filled the cave. The figure advanced and was revealed by the dim light coming from above. Will could see a maw filled with teeth like Ginsu knives. Blazing eyes. Little arms. A huge body.

Prey. No—not just prey. *The* prey. The reason the raptors had gathered here. This was the food he had smelled in the hills.

Will thought of the fissure he had seen when he and Junior had raced for the food, the telltale marks of an earthquake that must have ripped through this area—perhaps not all that long ago.

This was where the food had gone. This was where it had taken shelter, trying to throw off its hunters.

This was where it had been trapped.

Did Big Guy know about this? Did this have something to do with the "extinction event"—as Will was now thinking of it—scheduled for three days from now?

Will looked at the dinosaur before him and *felt* a seething hatred roll off the larger creature. The floor of the cave rocked as the dinosaur advanced toward him. It must have weighed a ton!

Will drew back. He didn't know what to do, or if there was anything he *could* do.

He gasped—and the dinosaur was upon him.

PART TWO

ACROCANTHOSAURUS: IMPOSSIBLE

CHAPTER 9

PATIENCE

Faster!

Patience was pushing herself hard. She'd been running ever since she'd scented food. The soggy land had given way to swamp as Mr. London writhed and squirmed, his tiny head whacking from side to side against Patience's roaring belly. He yelped and pleaded with her to slow down. But she couldn't. She had to stay focused, stay in the zone, or else—

Her stomach rumbled. And food was in her grasp.

"Yahhhh-ahhh-ahhh!" Mr. London cried, as if sensing her thoughts.

Patience frowned. Her teacher was acting like a baby, even though he looked like a writhing little beak-faced Gila monster. She stopped. A final splatter of mud splashed around her.

"Why'd you want to come with me if you were just gonna slow me down?" Patience asked. "You were the one who said I needed to get back to Zane as quick as I could, in case something came out of the dark and tried to eat him."

"I thought you might need help..."

Patience didn't think that was the reason. She was sure it had more to do with her teacher's all-consuming curiosity about this age. She dropped Mr. London onto a muddy flat, and he scampered away from her and started pacing.

The rain hadn't let up all evening. If anything, it was getting worse. And the collection of curving trees and canopies of reeds and vines that jutted from the muck offered very little protection.

"You don't know how hungry I'm feeling!" Patience roared as she stalked toward him, claws twitching.

"Gahhh!" Mr. London wailed. "I understand. I understand!"

Patience stopped. "So what is it you're after?"

"Food must be scarce in this region," Mr. London said. "And there must be a reason."

He took a deep breath and let it out. Mud sputtered from his nostrils. "Ugh."

"Ditto."

"I suppose the lack of food in this area could be due to a drought. Offhand, I wouldn't say that, considering this rain. But these downpours may have been sudden, coming at the end of a dry season. That's possible..."

"But that's not what you're worried about."

Mr. London shook his head. "There is the possibility of some widespread disease. I hope not, but it's something we have to consider. Bertram talked about an event that could change history.

"What most people fail to understand about the age of dinosaurs is that there were three extinction events—not just one—that wiped the dinosaurs from the face of the earth by the end of the late Cretaceous. That's why the Mesozoic is divided into three periods, Triassic, Jurassic, and Cretaceous."

Patience blinked, sniffing the air.

"We're in the mid-Cretaceous now," Mr. London continued. "There shouldn't be any major extinction event. But one good disease, carried over a far enough distance—"

"Are you worried that I'll eat something diseased, get sick, and bring the disease to Will and Ground Zero? That I'll cause whatever's going to happen?"

"Unwittingly. Yes."

"Great."

"It's just that we have to be very careful. We have to think before we act."

"Yeah, like you did with the machine."

He looked away. "Exactly my point."

Patience lowered her craggy head.

"What I scented did smell a little funny, but I didn't have any 'Danger, Will Robinson!' warnings coming from my inner dino,"she said.

"You're starved, I'm not. My instincts may be less unbiased."

"Fine." She looked around as a sudden fearful emptiness took hold of her. "The food! I can't smell it anymore!"

"It may have gone underwater."

"What, like one of those giant crocs in Bertram's story or something?" Patience thought about it. "I could go for a little crocburger."

"Croc *tartare* is more like it," Mr. London said. "No way to cook food. You'd have to eat it raw."

Patience looked at her teacher, her chest heaving. "It'd still be better than snarfing down something like you. I mean—look at the size of you! You'd be a chicken nugget. One single chicken nugget."

Patience's brain began to fog over. A desire stronger than any she had ever known gripped her.

Chick-en nug-get

She turned away quickly, hugging herself as best she could with her tiny little arms. The sail running along her spine shuddered and flapped in the wind.

Don't look at him, Patience thought. *Your teacher is not a chicken nugget!*

She bent low and ducked her head into the water. She couldn't see anything, but as the rancid water filled her sensitive nostrils, she detected something overripe, icky in the extreme, and—edible.

Patience yanked her head out of the water and looked at Mr. London. "I've got the scent back! The food's downstream."

She took off, carrying the quivering little Hypsilophodon. There was no sound but the buzz of insects over the steady drumming of the rain.

They moved through a tangled maze of reeds and

tree branches, bumping and slamming their way through every barrier in their path. The mud grew thicker in places, more slippery in others. Patience sloshed and teetered until they found what she had smelled. The food had been trapped underwater, where it had died. Its scent had been absorbed by the swamp.

"Carrion," Mr. London said. "Potentially ripe with disease. Did you know that predators such as yourself often came down with gout due to an overabundance of red meat in their diet?"

Patience drove Mr. London up against the food and held him there, kicking and struggling.

"Diseased?" she asked.

He spat. "No."

"Chow time." Patience couldn't see what the creature had been. For that, she was grateful. She set Mr. London on a thick branch and crouched over the drowned remains of whatever this thing had been.

"Don't look," Patience said. "And if I—lose it—"

"Running will not be an issue," Mr. London said. "I will do so happily."

"Thanks."

Patience let herself go. For the next few minutes, she was dimly aware of tearing, of crunching, of chewing, of food—wonderful food—filling her yearning, empty belly.

The sounds of the rain and the insects fell away

for a time. Then she found herself crouching in the waters, her senses returning to normal. A crunching, chomping sound came to her from somewhere close. Other Acros? Her head whipped around sharply. In the twisted cage of branches and reeds surrounding them, she saw movement.

"Gahhhh!" Mr. London cried, dropping a mouthful of soggy leaves. He raced along the branch, knocked his head into a tree trunk, and fell into the water below.

Patience fished him out with her maw and set him on a branch. "It's all right. We're fine."

"I thought—"

"I'm okay," Patience said. She smelled her own breath and nearly gagged as the tastes in her mouth overwhelmed her. Mr. London leaped into her waiting arms, and they trod back in the direction they had come from, Patience following the pull that told them they were moving toward their ultimate goal.

"You don't talk much, do you?" Mr. London asked.

"You say that like it's a bad thing."

"I noticed how quiet you were in class—when you weren't hitting anyone. I thought I was boring you."

Patience shrugged. "You were. You are. Any point to this?"

Mr. London fell silent.

Patience fought her way through the reeds and branches, smashing at them with her shoulders while she protected Mr. London. It made her think of the time she'd been lost in the woods when she was eight, after she'd run away from the orphanage.

She'd escaped to see Amy, a woman who had adopted her, then become gravely ill. That frantic night, Patience had heard a scratching and movement. Growing still, she'd picked up a fallen branch and stood ready to face whatever creature had been stalking her.

It was an orange-and-black-striped tabby. Conan.

They'd become fast friends. She had read to the frightened kitten from the book of Robert E. Howard stories that she carried around. She had pressed him against her, feeling the kitten's heartbeat, sensing when his fear ebbed, talking softly to him, and driving her own concerns away by protecting him.

Later that night, when Patience had been found, the cat was taken from her.

Patience shrugged off the past and looked down at the tiny creature in her arms. Mr. London's heart was beating like a trip-hammer. Just like Conan's...

"I'm sorry," Patience said as she pushed at a barrier of reeds. "I shouldn't have said that."

"I've hidden my tears before," Mr. London said in a lighter tone than she would have expected.

Patience shrugged. "If you can't find what you need inside yourself, you're looking in the wrong place."

"And you read that..."

"On a cereal box."

"Good cereal."

"I thought so."

"So you're content with your life?" Mr. London looked up. "I've never met anyone like that before. What's it like?"

Patience smashed into branches a lot harder than she had to and didn't put a great deal of effort into protecting Mr. London from the worst of it.

Then she stopped again. "What is with this place? I know I'm going in the right direction. I can feel it. But all these reeds and trees make it impossible to get anywhere."

"I don't know," Mr. London said. "I—glmmmphh!"

Patience felt Mr. London wriggling in her claws. She looked down to see him partially underwater. Patience lifted him up—and that's when she saw it. "Mr. L..."

Water drained from him as if he were a wet rag. "I see."

The waters were rising. The rains were flooding the swamp!

"We have to get out of here," Patience said. The waters were up past her belly and mounting quickly.

Mr. London leaped from her arms onto a low-hanging branch. "I'll get help!"

"Wait!" she said. But he left her—just like everyone else. Fine. She'd handle this on her own.

Patience surveyed the area. What little she could see reminded her of a maze. She was surrounded by tree-walls, some with spaces between them, some without.

She tried to mentally retrace her route—but she was lost. Patience looked down. The waters were higher now. And they would get higher still, very soon. She tried every path she could find. Battered at wall after wall. But she couldn't find her way back to land!

Soon the waters were splashing so high, the muck was going up Patience's nose. She pushed through a narrow passage between the walls and made a sharp turn. Another wall. She'd reached a dead end.

Patience clawed at a handful of reeds—and they broke off in her grip. She tried to hook her feet between a pair of trees, and they splintered under her weight. She launched herself against the wall, battered it, and screamed in fury.

Suddenly, she heard a tremendous splash from the other side of the wall, followed by a strangled cry.

"Patience!" Mr. London called. "Patience—glllrrrrppphhh!"

She stood back as a huge head came over the wall. The little dinosaur rode atop Zane's head! The brontosaurus smashed through the wall with his tree-trunk legs, then turned.

"His tail!" Mr. London yelped. "Grab his tail!"

Zane's tail whipped overhead as the rain slapped at her. Thunder roared and lighting rippled across the sky. She latched on to Zane's tail and fought to keep her head above water as he stomped through the swamp, smashing everything in his way to bring her to safety.

Soon they were on higher ground. Patience lay shuddering, staring at Zane and Mr. London. Runt peered down at them from a hill. The one who had some sense.

"You came back," Patience said. She had never been so stunned. No one ever came back. No one. And yet—they had!

Mr. London gazed at her, his tiny chest heaving, puffs of short, sharp breath leaving him.

"We're in this together," Mr. London said.

Patience nodded. For the first time, she actually believed it.

CHAPTER 10

WILL

Will awoke to find himself pinned down by an enormous dinosaur. It snored heavily.

HUNGRY–HUNGRY–HUNGRY

Cut that out! Will demanded in his head. The dinosaur that pinned him snorted and moved a little.

"Oh, boy," Will said with a sigh.

He remembered what had happened. The dinosaur had lunged at him, he had been slammed back, his head striking the wall, and there had been a blinding flash behind his eyes—and his memories ended there.

Now the dinosaur lay with the edge of its belly jamming him into place against the cave wall. Will wriggled to the side and felt some of the pressure ease. This thing weighed a ton! If it had fallen on him directly, it would have crushed him.

He had a sense that it was morning, though the light within this cavern had not changed. He guessed that his stomach counted the seconds between meals.

Carefully, Will eased himself out from under the dinosaur. It grunted but did not wake. He got as good a look at it as he could in the dull illumination from the stuff sticking to the ceiling. The dinosaur had been hurt. He could smell the freshness of its, no, *her*—wounds.

He had a vague memory of Mr. London reviewing a few of his favorite plant-eaters. If Will wasn't mistaken, she was one of them. A Tenontosaurus—the natural prey of raptor packs.

He looked around. The vast chamber in which he found himself had a high ceiling with sharp, jagged spikes of stone hanging from it, and other odd, twisting shapes rising up from the floor. There was only one spot in the cavern that might have been a tunnel entrance. The opening in the wall was too small for the heavy plant-eater to fit through, but Will could manage it if he ducked down first.

Maybe it was a way back to the others!

But did he really want to go? He'd tried to be popular, and for his crime he'd been hauled away and tossed out of the pack. What if Leiman had been right? If he was one of the elite, then at least he would be someone. And he'd know where he stood.

He heard the Tenontosaurus stirring. She moved faster than he would have expected, lunging at him again. He leaped out of the way, and the next thing he knew, she was sitting in front of the small tunnel entrance, blocking it with her bulk.

"You *want* me trapped in here with you?" Will asked.

A throaty growl left the Tenontosaurus.

"Perfect," Will muttered. He found his own patch of wall and leaned against it. This is how the elitists lived. Separate from all others, with no trust. Their backs to the wall.

It was *liberating*. There were no illusions. No one to impress. If he could just figure out a way to get past the leaf-eater...

He didn't smell any food in this chamber *except* her, and he didn't know how long he could control himself.

Maybe Big Guy would notice he was gone and send some raptors after him. Buddy and Binky—

A sudden memory brought him up short. Had they been with Junior and his Lost Boys last night? He dimly recalled faces like theirs. But it had been dark, chaotic. It couldn't have been them.

Wake up, Will, Briefcase Man said. *There must be something Tink over there wants...*

Will made a more thorough search of the walls and floor. He found roots and bits of greens growing through cracks in the cavern walls. He extracted all he could, carefully avoiding the guardian of the portal. Once he'd amassed a decent pile of greens, he backed off and waited for the Tenontosaurus to chow down.

The dinosaur didn't move.

Next Will made a trail of "bread crumbs" with the tasty-looking greens, getting as close as he dared to the wounded plant-eater. Finally, he lost his patience and tossed a handful of leaves into the Tenontosaurus's lap, then quickly backed away.

HUNGRY-HUNGRY-HUNGRY

Will whacked his head into the wall, hoping the pain would sweep away the natural urges he'd been fighting all night long.

REND-TEAR-RIP-SLASH

It took what felt like hours, but at last the Tenontosaurus ate the greens. Still, she didn't leave the portal. Will arced around the large dinosaur, trembling with hunger. He was tired and weak and *ravenous*. There'd been no sign of any of the ratlike creatures he'd hoped to find within the mountain.

ATTACK-ATTACK-EAT-EAT-EAT

No! He had to find some other way to get Tink away from the portal. All he had to work with was some roots, leaves, and the rock surrounding him.

Everything he needed to make a torch!

Will watched Tink carefully as he set to work. He used a stretch of hardened root for the handle, then wrapped leaves around the top and tied them in place with thin vines. Flint was easy to find.

Soon he was striking stones together until he had a spark. Tink stood and wailed as Will approached with his torch. She stood her ground as long as she could, then she leaped out of the way as Will lunged at her with the fire.

He plunged through the portal, hoping it was indeed a tunnel and not just a crevice. He ran ahead. The tunnel appeared endless. Yet he could smell *something*. The scent of the Tenontosaurus he'd left behind was still in his nostrils, but this was something else, something sweeter, riper.

He saw a ledge just ahead. The air was thinner now. There were little sounds. Screechings. Scratchings. Chirps. His instincts were screaming at him to leap forward—

HUNGRY-HUNGRY-HUNGRY

—because somewhere *down there* was *food!*

From his left, Will heard a trickle of water. He was *so* thirsty...Parched. So he followed what appeared to be a small shelf and soon beheld fresh water trickling down the side of the cavern through a hairline fracture in the mountain.

Nothing had *ever* tasted so wonderful!

Muzzle still wet, Will turned to find a massive cavern so huge the torch barely began to light it. He could see needle-like twisting swords of stone above that looked like rows of teeth from some ancient leviathan. Glistening water on those sharp projections reflected the firelight, giving the cavern a magical feel, as if it were lit by twinkling candles set in high chandeliers.

Then he saw the dark pit that lay directly before him and the irregular, gap-ridden ledge circling it. To his immediate left, just past the little fountain, was a four-foot hole in the ledge—a sharp and possibly deadly drop-off.

But to the right, the ledge held for quite a way. He traced it and came to a group of stones piled up from the pit below. If they held, he'd be able to climb down them to reach whatever was skittering, crawling, squealing—

FOOD-FOOD-FOOD

—below.

He shone the torch into the abyss and saw hordes of tiny green salamander-like things and—rats! It looked like the floor, a good fifteen feet below, was *crawling* with food. He wanted to just jump down and devour, but he had to consider one important fact.

What if he couldn't leap high enough to reach the ledge once more?

He had to test the rock ladder. He climbed down as gracefully as he could, reached the bottom, and snatched up a handful of the wriggling green sallies.

Ugh-oh, they're still moving, yuck.

But he was *HUNGRY-HUNGRY-HUNGRY*.

And with so many succulent treats waiting, he *flung* himself at the buffet.

Afterward, Will looked around and saw several more branching tunnels. *There might be a way out.*

The thought frightened him.

He tried to picture himself searching through those tunnels alone. If what lay ahead was anything like the video games he played with his buddies, those tunnels could lead to an ever more complex maze. He might never find his way back. Then he'd really be alone. He wouldn't even have Tink to keep him company.

On the other hand, there was the rescue party to think about. He had no idea what dinosaurs they might be inhabiting. Other raptors, hopefully. If not, they could easily end up as prey. He had to escape this place and meet them before they reached the valley.

From her chamber, Tink wailed. It was a high, mournful cry.

There was no water where she'd been trapped. Will knew it wasn't his problem. But...

She wailed again.

Sighing, he turned back. His explorations would have to wait.

CHAPTER 11

ZANE

He stood in a winding valley, buffeted by shrieking winds and hissing rain. He stared at the sleet-gray sky.

Mr. London had gone off to make the acquaintance of a group of wildly colored Iguanodons he'd spotted several miles away. Patience hadn't liked the idea of stopping, but she owed Mr. London big-time, so she kept her mouth shut. Runt, thankfully, had chosen to nap.

Normally, Zane didn't like to have time on his hands to think. Especially on days when the weather was like this. It reminded him too much of the last time he'd seen his dad.

He'd gone off to work at the insurance company, acting like everything was fine. But he had never come back. Instead, he had sent movers for his things. No good-byes...

"Hey."

Zane swung his head around.

"Sorry," Patience said. "Didn't mean to scare you."

"Wasn't scared," Zane said. It wasn't a lie, even though his heart thundered and his belly and legs shook. Scared was too mild a word.

"I'm not really good at thank-yous," Patience said, "but—thank you."

"No prob!" Zane said. "We're all here to help each other, right?"

Patience looked down and tried to force her tongue between a pair of jagged, broken teeth. Something was stuck there. It appeared to be a bone.

"Look, I've been thinking," Patience said softly. "I may have been a little harsh with Will. You know, back in the lunchroom." She hesitated. "You know about all that, right? You were in on it. Or am I wrong?"

Zane hesitated. "The girly-girl thing?"

She nodded.

"Not my idea. For once."

"He really wasn't trying to set me up? It really wasn't about me at all? I mean, besides using me. If I said okay."

"He didn't want to hurt you, no."

"I think I got so mad because he was right," Patience said. "I *do* want to get back at Monique. I would like to shut her up. It's just the idea that I'm so easy, that someone could figure me out—"

"Lance," Zane said quickly. "It was Lance."

"Whoever. I want to give it a try."

Zane bobbed his head in confusion. "Okay. So why are you telling me?"

"You're the one with the four sisters. Teach me."

He raised his head a little, looking to see if anyone else was around. Then he turned back to Patience. "You're serious?"

"Yeah."

Zane saw some *serious* possibilities for fun. And for a little payback. "If we do this, I'm the one in charge. You do what I say, and you don't start in about eating me again."

"Right."

He was starting to *like* this. He looked over to the rocky ledge, where Mr. London had left the amber key. Zane had promised to watch over it.

"All right, recruit," Zane said. "Let's go!"

Half an hour later, Zane was eating it up. And Patience was trying. Really trying.

He could tell that she meant it when she told him she wouldn't have him for lunch, no matter what he asked of her. Of course, that had been before he had started teaching her *how* to *walk*.

A heavy stone sat on her Acrocanthosaurus skull. Her shoulders were thrust back, her chest out, her chin held high. And—

"Back straight," Zane urged. "Are you serious about this or what?"

Patience growled. She walked on, the wind howling like a pack of mocking kids.

Oooooooooohhhhh—look at the tomboy trying to be a girly-girl—oooooooooohhhhhhh.

Zane *almost* felt for her.

So far, she had been able to walk a hundred feet without losing the rock. That was her record. She was close to bettering that record now, just a few more steps—

The rock fell. It made a low *plop* as it hit the mud. Patience roared, picked it up, and tossed it a dozen feet. Chest heaving, she stood trembling, head down, eyes shut.

"This is *not* working!" she cried.

"You wanna drop out, just say the word."

Ooohhh, ain't I a stinker, Zane thought. *I'm actually enjoying this.*

Patience's shoulders slumped. "Sorry."

"I don't think you're serious about this."

"I am!"

He shrugged, staring into a little puddle, practicing funny faces with his big shuddering camel lips. He'd always been rubber-faced, but now...

Patience gently dipped her tail into the water, making his image bubble and ripple away. "Come on," she urged. "I really want to do this."

Zane raised his long neck and squinted. "Then give me the litany."

She shuddered. "Not that."

"Can't have it both ways."

She sighed and began her recitation. "Girls do not fight. Girls do not swear. At least, not when boys are around. Girls don't act too smart. Girls don't get in trouble with the teacher. Everything a guy says—"

"I'm not getting that personal feeling."

Patience gritted her teeth. "Everything my guy tells me is the most amazing thing I've ever heard, and every joke he tells is the funniest joke I could ever imagine, even if it's really lame. And whatever movie he wants to see is the one I'm really interested in seeing, too."

"More." Zane was making new funny faces.

"Girly-girls hang back. They're not too forceful with their opinions. And—"

"And they don't think of themselves as 'girly-girls.' Or use that phrase out loud."

"Right."

Zane started moving again. His head swayed over the ground, searching for something. "Seriously, Patience," he said. "It's not a crime to have a feminine side. Everybody does. You, me, Will. Yin-yang, male-female, strong-sensitive. Okay?"

"*You* don't have to wear dresses."

"I would if it'd get me on national TV!" Zane said. "It worked for Tom Hanks. Now sashay with the hips. I want to see some sway, bounce, *boo-tay*..."

She swung her tail around.

"The hips, the hips!"

She did it. She looked like she hated it, but she did it. "What does this make my butt look like?"

"Ask me again when we get home. Now up on the tippy-toes. You've got to get used to that if you're going to wear heels."

Patience ground to a stop. "Heels?"

"Heels. Flats and a dress? Unh-uh. I don't think so." He was still scanning the ground.

"Zane, what are you doing?" she finally asked.

"Lookin' for something."

"Like what?"

"Flint."

Patience nodded. "You want to start a fire?"

"Does it have to be flint for that?" Zane asked. "And what does flint look like, anyway?"

Sighing, Patience said, "We're not talking about any practical purpose here, are we? I mean, you're not thinking, oh, if we had torches and somehow protected them from the rain, we could cover more territory at night, or we could make watch fires, or something useful like that, are you?"

Zane's long neck drooped a little. "Not exactly."

Psssssst—bbrmmmmph-BROOF!

A cloud of noxious fumes drifted their way. They both looked at Runt, whose backside shuddered as he pranced around.

Patience shoved her craggy skull close to Zane's. The sail along her back tensed and stood straight up, despite the wind. "You were thinking of lighting up one of his—"

"Yah."

She growled, "That's just wrong! What could you possibly be thinking?"

Zane's head wobbled. "It'd be funny."

"You'd scare him so bad we'd never get him back!"

They stared at each other for a moment, considering...

"That's just wrong," Patience said firmly.

"Well, I would have needed your help, anyway," Zane said, raising one of his massive feet. "See. Loss of manual dexterity is an issue."

Patience found a rock and beat her head against it. Runt came over, tried it, found he didn't like it, and wandered off.

"Come on, Patience," Zane said. "You've gotta practice your girly-girlies if you want to—"

He froze.

"What?" Patience asked.

Zane was looking at the ledge where they'd left the amber key.

It was gone.

"Mr. London!" Zane hollered. *"Mr. London!"*

Patience stood, sniffing at the air. "The wind was pushing at us, taking our scent back to whatever snatched the key. That's how it got so close."

"Uh-huh," he said, totally panicked.

Patience walked for a few minutes. "I've got its scent! It was another Acro!"

Patience pointed at a fork not far back in the path. "I bet it came from around there. I can track it, but I'll have to go alone!"

"Alone?" Zane said. He tried to keep the quiver out of his voice.

This could be a trap, Zane thought. *One Acro could be trying to lead you away so we'll be unprotected when the others arrive!*

"Patience, don't!" he hollered.

But she was already out of sight.

CHAPTER 12

PATIENCE

Patience followed the thief's trail for nearly two hours. It led her to a high hill overlooking a vast encampment of Acrocanthosaurus. The rain had tapered off, and the yellow light of midmorning shone down like a beacon.

The Acrocanthosaurus clan gathered in a valley fitted with winding corridors and vast chambers, rocky overhangs and steep rises. Patience was reminded of an image from a picture book she had been given at the orphanage—a book of mazes.

She watched. Things were quiet enough. The Acros moved around from chamber to chamber, meeting up, hanging out. Not exactly what she had expected. Maybe this was their downtime.

Somewhere in the encampment was the amber key—or so her nose told her. All the scents led here.

She steeled herself for a fight as she broke from cover and headed down a trail that led to the encampment. She couldn't imagine why they had taken the amber key. What use would it be to them?

Her best guess was that it had been taken by good old Number 47. That dinosaur was down there with the others, along with the Green Knight—the dinosaur who'd taken a bite out of Zane earlier.

Seeing him again created in her a longing she'd rarely felt. It must have had something to do with her inner dino.

Acros in love. Great.

As Patience moved moved down the hill, she thought about her earlier decision to take "girly-girl" lessons from Zane and wondered if her host had influenced her.

No. She was after Monique, plain and simple.

If Number 47 was like Monique, she'd be drawn to any bright, shiny object. And if she had somehow sensed how important the key was to Patience, that would have added to the allure.

If someone says I can't have something, that's the best reason to want it. Which was exactly what Monique would think. The stuck-up, lousy little—

Patience reached the bottom of the hill and tried to control her emotions. She was going into battle. She had to get herself in the zone...

A group of four Acros looked up as she approached. Patience felt a pull far stronger than the other-worldly sense that told her if she was heading toward or away from Ground Zero.

And she'd felt that pull before.

The Acros stared at her—then one broke from the group and rushed her!

Patience remembered the "game" of dominance and submission she had been forced to play with Number 47. This time, she would have to be the one to back down. And *that* would be the challenge for her: to defy her instincts and allow herself to be bent to the will of another. Patience bristled at the thought but knew it was the only way to infiltrate the Acrocanthosaurus clan and find the amber key.

But something was wrong. Her inner dinosaur wasn't feeling the least bit defensive. In fact, the feelings rising up were the warm and fuzzy kind.

Had she snapped? The Acro running toward her flung herself at Patience, her sail wriggling, her little arms open wide. The pair fell to the earth with a loud thud. The other Acro nuzzled Patience and made a low, vibrating sound, almost like a purr!

What was going on here?

The other Acro rolled off Patience, allowing her to get up and face the welcoming committee, which had sauntered over. Not one attacked. In fact, they all appeared excited to see her!

Strangest of all, she felt *happy* to see them. That's what that the pull had been about. The odd feeling she'd experienced was bliss.

Patience allowed the dinosaurs to lead her to one of the larger chambers. She saw at once that the patterns of their markings were similar to hers. Was this how they decided if another Acro was friendly or hostile? Stripes with stripes, spots with spots?

But there had been plenty of others who looked nothing like this group, and there had been no conflicts that she had seen. A throaty growl sounded. Patience turned and saw Number 47.

Now it starts, Patience thought. Number 47 stalked forward, hissing angrily. Two of the Acros surged toward 47, growling and snapping their maws. Number 47 whined, whimpered, and backed off.

Patience laughed. "Now I *like* this."

Number 47 disappeared, her tail dragging. After Patience was sniffed, nuzzled, and even *cuddled* by the first group of Acros, she heard footsteps and looked up to see another batch of dinosaurs approaching from the inner reaches of the labyrinth.

The Green Knight was not with them. Patience felt a little disappointed.

These Acros were different sizes and sported varied spots, stripes, and splotches on their scales. All welcomed her.

It was weird, but it was exactly what Patience had come down here to achieve. The Acros accepted her.

"I guess we're all friends," Patience said.

The Acros sniffed and nuzzled her. Yep. Well, as

nice as all this was, Patience still had a mission to accomplish. One of the Acros had taken the amber key, and she had to get it back.

"You guys don't mind if I just kind of check out the place, do you?" Patience asked.

The other Acros followed along as Patience entered the corridor leading to the heart of the maze. They crowded around her, making it difficult for Patience to check out all the little crevices in which the key might have been stowed. But she managed.

Every now and then she heard a crunch beneath her. Looking down, she saw twigs and branches blown here by high winds. There were also bones. Patience examined a nearby skeleton. It had been a *shark*.

The Acros moved from room to room. She'd started thinking of the spaces as rooms now, not chambers or cells. And this place really wasn't much of a labyrinth. All Patience had to do was follow the cardinal rule of any maze and she could easily find her way around. Pick one direction or the other, right or left, and bear that way the whole time.

Besides, this place seemed familiar. More like a home. A cozy communal dwelling.

But there was no hint of the amber key. She pictured dogs burying bones in backyards and worried about how impossible her task might prove to be.

Then she felt it. A fiery attraction from two rooms

ahead. The key!

She was in the zone now. That place beyond worry and fear. Passing a long corridor, Patience came to a room where she sensed she would find the stolen treasure.

It was a room unlike all the others. It had a high, rocky ledge and a roof that would provide partial shelter from storms.

She'd been able to see into this room from the hill. She recalled dinosaurs moving through it but not remaining. It was near the center of the maze, the biggest room of all. Surprisingly, it was occupied.

The Green Knight stood before her. He lowered his head and took a step back as she approached. A knight bowing before his lady.

Her sail rustled slightly.

Patience studied every corner of the room, digging around in the shadowy place. The key wasn't there, but that odd feeling remained. Why?

A pair of Acrocanthosaurs appeared from the opposite end of the room. Patience scented them and guessed that they were older than the others. The mother and father of the clan.

Another old TV show came to mind. One the Mushnicks watched constantly in reruns.

They were the Bradys. Mike and Carol.

It was beginning to make sense. Many of these

dinosaurs were related. Children. Nieces, nephews, cousins. Other families and friends. This was a welcoming place for all. A place of love and kindness. Acceptance and understanding. It was—

A roar came from behind Patience. She turned just in time to see Number 47 rush at her. The Green Knight slammed 47 against the wall.

Mom and Pop Brady growled at her. Number 47 mewled and whined and stamped her feet.

You like her better. You let her get away with everything! She can hang out with plant-eaters, do whatever she wants!

This gaudily scaled dinosaur wasn't the favored daughter, she wasn't Marcia. She was *Jan*. Number 47 was Jan Brady!

Oh, Monique, this is what you deserve, it really is.

Patience started laughing. Then Mike and Carol came over to sniff, nuzzle, and welcome her. Unlike the others, they made her feel special. It was a connection she had dreamed of all her life.

"I can't believe this," Patience whispered, fighting her instinct.

She wasn't a *friend* to this clan. She was a *part* of it. And the dinosaurs standing in front of her were her *parents*.

CHAPTER 13

PATIENCE

Suddenly, Patience broke from the embrace of the elder Acros.

"No," Patience said, backing away. She didn't want this. She had come only looking for the key.

She tried to run—but there was nowhere to go. Two corridors led from this room. One was blocked by her mother and father. The other was clogged by a host of Acrocanthosaurus. She could feel her connection to them. Her brothers and sisters. Greg. Bobby. Cindy. Peter...

There was something else. This was her room. A private place she could come whenever she wanted. A safe place. Somewhere *she* belonged.

"No," Patience said, backing away. She didn't want this. She had come only looking for the key.

She thought of the great chamber where Mom and Pop Brady lived. In a blur she sped around them and raced down the corridor to their room. In it, she found some heavy rocks and the trunk of an overturned tree that had been blasted into toothpicks.

She searched, grasping, clawing at the walls, digging in the dirt. There was no key.

She heard a chuffing sound behind her. Mom and Dad. They were curious and concerned.

"You can't be my parents," Patience whispered. "I won't let you..."

She thought of the department store when she was three. The faceless woman who abandoned her. Then Amy, who found her and swore they would always be together, until Amy's sickness came and Patience ended up in the orphanage.

Patience straightened up. All right. This body she was in had parents. *It* had a family. That had *nothing* to do with her.

Besides, this family would be like all the others. Wonderful at first glance, but something entirely different once she really got to know them.

"I'm here for the key," Patience said. She clung to the image of the key, placing it at the forefront of her thoughts. She concentrated so hard that she suddenly felt as if her thoughts were too much for her to contain. They burst from her, exploding like stars, reaching out.

Patience immediately realized what was happening. With the exception of occasionally touching the feelings radiating from creatures around her, she had refused to use her own psychic gifts. Now they were released in full force, projecting the image of the amber key and her desire to recover it into the minds of every Acro nearby!

Patience broke the connection, but not before she sensed an overwhelming desire to help, a desire that came from the dinosaurs around her.

She shuddered. *You want to help Marcia. Not me. None of it has anything to do with me.*

But maybe she could use that to her advantage. She saw Number 47 skulking near the door. Patience was certain that 47 was the one who'd taken the key.

Patience growled at 47. The dinosaur glared, and Patience recognized that look. The little thief wasn't about to give up her prize.

"Okay, everybody!" Patience cried. "Marcia's back! Let's have a cookout or something to celebrate!"

Mom and Pop Brady immediately picked up on her change of tone. All the Acros danced around happily. All except Number 47.

Score.

Patience was led outside. She heard some grumbling and realized it was the stomachs of her fellow Acros. She was hungry, too. She sniffed, wondering if the scent of her companions was still on her. Would the other Acros expect her to lead them to Mr. London, Zane, and Runt?

But the group headed off in the opposite direction. Patience saw hills in the distance. As they walked, the younger Acros happily chased one another while Mom and Pop Brady looked on.

Patience glanced back to see Number 47 trailing the group, her head down, her eyes glaring.

They passed through a darkened tunnel at the base of the closest hill. It twisted and turned and was filled with terrible smells. Patience couldn't see where she was going, but she had a natural sense of the correct path. Her host dinosaur must have walked through here many times. The dank odors blocked any scents that might have come from the other side of the hill.

They turned a corner, and the tunnel's mouth came into view. Beyond it, Patience heard rushing water. She walked through the opening and was thrilled to see the gray shore of a lake and a great river flowing ino it.

The opposite shore was only a hundred yards away. Huge rocks and islands of debris acted as stepping stones across the water.

Patience saw a magnificent waterfall cutting through another range of high hills. Clouds of frothing water mixed with the river at its base. Around her, the wind howled and moaned, and light rain fell. It should have felt dreary and depressing, but instead, the chill in the air was invigorating.

The Acros began to fish. They took positions along the waves and studied the water. When a school of fish came into view, they pounced. Pop Brady dropped too far forward and fell in!

Patience laughed as he bounced along the bottom of the shallow river, keeping his snout above water, and climbed up on the shore. She considered going in and fishing with the others, but she had an idea of what might happen if she stood apart and let the others do the work.

The Green Knight was the first to arrive with an offering. A mawful of fish. Others came, including a pair bearing a shark. Patience watched 47 eat. The creature stomped to the shore and turned her backside to Patience as she looked for food.

After the fishing trip, Pop Brady took Patience for a walk. Number 47 followed, keeping her distance. Near the roaring base of the waterfall, they turned and walked along a marshy area.

Patience burped unexpectedly and tried to bring her little claw to her mouth. It didn't reach.

"Excuse me."

Pop Brady leaned in and nuzzled her. Patience saw Number 47 tremble with rage.

Everything was going according to plan. Yet...

Patience looked at the older Acro. "Can't you sense that I'm different? This body might belong to your daughter, but I'm not her. She's—I don't know where she is. Sleeping, I guess."

Pop Brady glanced at her with a peaceful expression. He accepted her completely. Number 47 growled, disrupting the tranquil mood.

They returned to the group. Mom was tending to a pack of young Acros, newly hatched and living in a mound about a mile west of the encampment. The smallest were only seven feet long, their sails mere bumps on their spines.

The parents stood nearby, allowing Mom Brady to feed their children. She motioned to Patience, who joined her and watched. Mom Brady allowed a number of fish to rest half in and half out of her mouth. She leaned in and waited until one of the little ones snapped a fish from her.

Patience loved it. "Looks like a fun game!"

Mom Brady nudged Patience toward the nearby pile of fish.

She scanned the area. Number 47 was nowhere in sight. Weird. Patience had been trying to make her "sister" so jealous that Number 47 would produce the thing she had taken to prove that she, too, was special: the amber key. She didn't expect the other dinosaur to pull a vanishing act.

Maybe she's gone to get the key, Patience thought. So there was no reason to feed the young. Her audience had gone. Patience heard tiny little mews. A chuffing. And a sneeze. The little dinosaurs cooed and chomped their maws, looking for more food.

Well, she didn't see any *harm* in feeding them.

Patience followed Mom Brady's example. It tickled when the young snatched the food from her mouth!

Suddenly, a chorus of cries sounded from the marshy area they'd left behind. Patience raced back with her mother.

They found Number 47 up to her middle in mud, thrashing around wildly. The Green Knight was on one side of the muddy pit that had trapped her, Pop Brady on the other.

Just had to have the attention, didn't you?

Then Patience realized this was no act. Number 47 was terrified. Patience studied the shifting muddy ground and saw tiny ratlike mammals scurry over its surface. With a snarl, Number 47 lunged and snapped at one of them, sinking deeper into the mud that pulled her down like quicksand!

If Number 47 was swallowed up by the mud, the key would be lost with her. And—

Number 47 was her sister.

Patience shook herself. She heard Acros coming from all around. In the mud, Number 47 splashed, snapped, and roared!

"You're making it worse!" Patience yelled. She thought of the way Number 47 had been treated by the Bradys. They weren't likely to help, even if they knew how. Every experience she ever had with families told Patience that, when it came down to it, everyone was on their own.

It was up to her. She had to—

Pop Brady took a step into the mud. Mom pressed up against his side and held his claws. The Green Knight circled around and took Mom's claws.

The Green Knight held his claws out to Patience, who was so surprised at what was unfolding before her that she took his claws without thinking. Another Acrocanthosaurus took hers. Then another, and another after that.

Patience saw other Acros approaching. Starting with Patience, they formed lines in front of and behind the chain of dinosaurs, pushing up against them, anchoring the Acrocanthosaurus.

Pop Brady stepped down into the mud trap. He sank quickly, but his mate held on. The Green Knight held on. So did Patience. She looked at the fierce determination in the eyes of the Green Knight and Mom and Pop Brady. Patience held on as she felt the earth beneath her go soft.

Number 47 had stopped struggling. Sharp little cries sounded from deep within her as her father came closer, his claws stretched out as far as his arm would allow.

"It's all right," Patience said. "It's—"

At the sound of her voice, 47 shrieked and howled. She struggled and attempted to lunge at Patience. She sank!

"No!" Patience yelled, and the creature calmed.

Patience watched as Number 47 was yanked from the mud, her claws flailing! As Pop Brady grabbed her, a terrible weight was suddenly added to the dinosaur chain. Patience sank in mud up to her hips, along with the dinosaurs anchoring her. She felt as if she was in the middle of a scaly, leathery group hug.

The Acrocanthosaurus in front of Patience slipped, and she clamped down with her jaws on his shoulder to steady him. He howled in pain, then regained his footing. She let go as the entire chain moved away from the mud trap, pulling Number 47 with them.

A half-dozen steps more, and they were free!

The chain fell apart. Number 47 dropped to her side, spitting out muck. Mom and Pop Brady stayed near, patting and nuzzling her.

Patience studied the circle of concerned dinosaurs and tried to take in what she had seen. She had been a part of the rescue effort. One part, nothing more. A link in the chain. She felt waves of love and concern from all the dinosaurs. Despite how bad Number 47 acted, she was *family*. Nothing could change that.

Her parents weren't two-faced *Bradys* at all. They had been willing to risk their lives to save one of their own. And so had she.

The Green Knight tromped up to her. He raised his snout and nodded toward a path a few yards away. Patience was nuzzled and hugged by several Acros as she started off in his direction. She turned and looked at her parents. They tilted their heads in unison, then closed their eyes slowly and nodded.

Go with him.

Patience needed to think. Her plan to make Number 47 return the key had failed.

Strangely, though she knew what was at stake, her sense of urgency had vanished. As she walked along a high, winding path that led to a pinnacle on their side of the waterfall, Patience thought about what Holiday had told her when she'd discovered her talent for hoops.

It's really something when you find something you didn't know you were looking for, something you never would have thought was lost.

Patience climbed the hill with the Green Knight and followed him to a huge stone ring. The rain fell harder, and the winds became stronger. The waterfall was beautiful. And for some reason, Patience felt just the slightest bit like a girly-girl out on a date!

"What is this? A make-out spot or something?"

The Green Knight fell to one knee and dug at the earth. Then he stood and motioned for Patience to come close.

At the base of the stone ring lay a collection of bright rocks and crystals. At the heart lay the amber key.

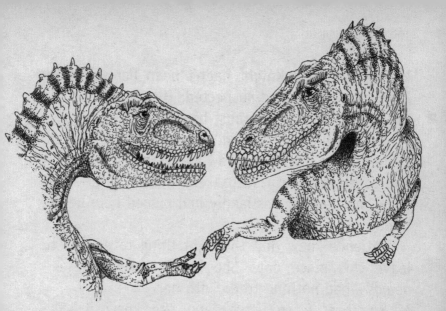

"*You* took it!" she cried. "Why?"

She bent down and reached for it. The Green Knigt's claws descended quickly. The Acros touched the amber key at the same instant. Images burned in Patience's mind.

Memories.

A bright, sunny afternoon, Patience nuzzling the Green Knight, only to have him reject her attentions. Nights when she'd tried to get close to him, only to have him act as if she were beneath his notice. Hunts on which she had gathered food and tried to share it with him, only to be ignored.

The memories faded. Patience found the key in her palm.

"What was that?" she asked. But some part of her

knew. The Green Knight hadn't been her suitor for long, not as she had suspected. His attentions had nothing to do with her host body.

It was all about her. *She* was the one he wanted. He had taken the key to draw her to the encampment and to place it with keepsakes—mating gifts—that other members of her family had placed here before him.

Patience knew that the right thing to do was to leave this place now. She had the key. These— *beings*—had nothing to do with her.

But that wasn't true, and she knew it. She reached out to the Green Knight, her arm trembling. Their claws nearly touched.

She belonged here. She *belonged*.

"I'm so tired," she whispered.

The Green Knight looked from her to the key, then to the little nest of baubles.

"No," she said. "I have to take this with me. I need it. We need it. There are others...another, well, not family, but *others*. I have to think about them. About everyone where I come from."

He looked at her again, his dark eyes alive with hope.

"No. Not now."

The Green Knight glanced toward the waterfall.

"If things don't work out, if we end up staying here, I'll come back. I can't promise anything else."

He chuffed.

Patience shook her head. "Like you can even understand a single word I'm saying."

He turned to her, and in that instant she knew that he *did* understand. Something had passed between them. Her words might have been lost on him, but what she felt inside had come through clearly.

They walked together for a time, heading far from the waterfall and the other Acros. Then they descended to the base of the steep hill.

"Hold on," Patience said with a yawn. "I need to rest. Just for a minute."

The Green Knight sat beside her. Patience stared up at the shimmering stars, and it wasn't long before she found herself resting her head on the other dinosaur's chest.

I'll go soon, Patience thought. *I just need to rest.*

Lying there, she felt that same sensation she'd experienced the first time she touched the key.

Home. It really did feel like home.

Smiling to herself, Patience fell into a deep, restful sleep.

CHAPTER 14

WILL

Will set his torch in an alcove. He gathered an armful of leaves and softer roots soaked in fresh water, then approached the dim glow at the end of the tunnel.

Tink was nowhere in sight, though he had seen her on the other side of the opening a short time before.

"Hey, Tink!" he called. "Got something for ya!"

A low moan of fear reverberated through the tunnel.

"Come on," Will said. "I'm *not* gonna hurt you!"

The moan rose.

Will darted his head through the opening, yelped, and pulled back swiftly. He moved just fast enough to avoid the swipe of a heavy claw.

Tink had been suckering him!

Water dripped from the leaves and the mass of roots he'd collected. He tossed the whole moist mess into the cavern and stepped into the darkness.

Tink came around, sniffing the leaves. She fell upon them quickly, licking at the wet ground where they'd fallen. Then she looked at Will and snarled.

"Yeah, you're welcome!" he said. "And don't forget to vote. Go with what you know."

He stared at the dinosaur. What an ingrate. It had actually been *hard work* getting back up to this level. Did she appreciate it? No. She tried to take his head off. She might as well have been a member of the Wetherford student body!

Will had been trying not to think about the election. But the defeat was still with him.

Along with something Lance had said...

I've invested—we've invested too much to let it end here.

Will had been too upset to make anything of his friend's remark at the time. But the more he thought about it, the edgier he became.

He considered Leiman, and how he had known so much of what was really going on. All the talk about being clear where you stand with people and not leaning on others—had he been trying to *warn* Will that his "buddy" might have been using him? Or had Leiman been trying to drive a wedge between Will and his friend?

Tink roared and tried to squeeze her way into the tunnel to get at Will.

Will sighed. He was trapped. But at least he knew where he stood...

Will turned his back on the Tenontosaurus. After gathering new kindling for his torch, he restored its dying fire. Then he went exploring.

He descended to the lizard pit again, then chose a branching tunnel at random. He used his sickle claw to mark X's on the wall as he went.

The network of tunnels became confusing. He went with Y's, Z's, then began with A's, marking each path separately but in a recognizable order. Sometimes he came to huge chambers with high ceilings. Other times he had to crawl to keep going.

He was descending into the lower depths of the mountain. Passages twisted and wound about, but they always led downward.

How far down, he couldn't say. Will *hoped* that he was now at ground level with the outside world, but he had no way of telling. The air was thinning, and his torch was flickering.

He stumbled over a fallen stalactite. He looked up at the array of shattered stalactites above. He thought about the earthquake that must have struck this area recently. If it happened again while he was inside the mountain, he could be trapped, or even crushed!

Chill, he commanded himself. He had to find a way out, and so he would. That was all.

Will came to a level area and began exploring one chamber after another. He had now used up the entire alphabet and was adding numbers to the letters he carved.

An odd smell came to him. Something sour just ahead. It made his lungs ache, his head hurt. His torch flickered again.

Will leaned against a wall, and a figure sprang at him. It was shorter than he was, with flashing teeth and wild eyes. The dinosaur had the scent of another meat-eater, but it *wasn't* a raptor. His torch was knocked from his hand, struck the ground, and fizzled out.

Will lashed out with a kick, his sickle claw extended. There was a yowl, then fading footsteps as whatever had attacked him retreated in the darkness.

He dropped to his knees and found his torch. He was lost in absolute darkness, but something told him not to relight the torch.

The bad smell intensified. He crawled forward. The smell grew worse.

Natural gas sometimes collected in mines. The same thing could have happened here. Maybe that was the bad smell...

Will rose to his feet and moved as quickly as he could. He struck a wall and felt around until he was able to leave the noxious chamber behind. The air cleared, and Will was heading downward again. He started marking his path again and relit the torch. This time, he'd put it out at the first whiff of gas.

The predator that attacked him had actually saved his life. If Will had walked through that chamber with his torch blazing, he would never have walked out again. He'd have been incinerated.

Of course, now he was *lost*.

Will walked on. The descent became steeper, but the air was sweeter. He turned a corner and was overwhelmed by delectable smells!

He felt *HUNGRY-HUNGRY-HUNGRY*.

It was Tink's scent. But how? She was back in the chamber, with no way out.

Another step, and the earth gave way beneath him. Will tumbled down a winding corridor, his torch sparking until it went out. He held on to it.

When he finally struck ground, Will became aware of a dull green light. He heard movement. His instincts *demanded* that he race forward and feed.

Instead, he dug his claws into the earth, fighting his urges until he had them under control. The scent of prey was strong here. It set his brain on fire!

He saw dim forms moving about. Some were as small as the shadowy figure that had knocked the torch from his hand, others were as large as Tink.

As his eyes adjusted, he saw that the dinosaurs were gathered by an underground stream. He heard moans, chirps, growls, and an odd trilling. Lumbering footfalls grew louder. The prey had spotted *him*.

He groped and found a pair of rocks. He struck them together three times, and a spark re-ignited his torch. A flame leaped into existence, revealing a crowded cavern with a domed ceiling.

An entire herd of Tenontosaurus had been trapped here. They were the prey the raptors had been hunting when they came to this valley.

A trio of huge dinosaurs advanced on him.

"Whoa! Hold on!" Will called.

They kept coming. He thought of Tink's warm reception, then turned and ran!

Getting away from them was easy. Will found a

tunnel too small for them to move through and darted inside. He ran uphill for a time, then slowed.

Just as his legs started to burn and ache, the
ground leveled out. He searched the walls, hoping to
find one of his marks.

It was there! He could trace his way back to the
lizard room, and from there he could try every other
branching tunnel.

One *had* to lead to the outside!

Will journeyed back, thinking about Tink. He had
misjudged her. She hadn't been an ingrate.

Tink had been *courageous*. She had placed herself
over the opening to keep a predator from reaching
the others. But what about the *other* predator he'd
encountered? Were there more of his kind in the tunnels, quietly hunting the Tenontosaurus who strayed
from the herd?

*Could this herd have something to do with Ground
Zero?* he wondered.

Will stopped. He was near the lizard room. He
could hear Tink roaring!

He scrambled up the stone ladder, nearly toppling
it in his haste. He circled the pit's ledge and ran
down the tunnel to Tink's chamber.

Inside, he found Tink standing on trembling legs,
staring up at a figure bursting through the same high
gap that had brought Will to her.

Yiiiiiaaaarrr-hsssssssssss—yip-yip-yip

Another raptor's head emerged from the opening, his jaws snapping hungrily as he sighted Tink.

Junior!

The raptor burst through the opening and fell to the ground. Will unsheathed his sickle claws, not altogether certain what he might do if Junior attacked Tink. Or him.

Instead, the raptor hissed and spat! One of his legs was twisted beneath him, and Will saw something lying near it—one of Junior's sickle claws. It had broken off in the fall.

The raptor rose on one leg and glared at Will as if his injury—his *crippling* injury—had been Will's fault.

"Junior" no longer seemed like a reasonable name for this maddened and dangerous creature. Will knew exactly what he was *really* facing:

Hook.

The raptor snarled and leaped!

CHAPTER 15

PATIENCE

Patience woke to her first glimpse of sunlight since she'd arrived in the age of dinosaurs. Massive gray storm clouds were scattered across the horizon. Bursting from between a pale cluster of them was a bold streak of fiery sunlight.

The amber key was still clutched firmly in her claw. She wouldn't lose it again. It was far too precious to her now.

Her head rested against the Green Knight's chest. He was snoring. Patience giggled. She couldn't help herself.

She was studying the sunlight glistening on his green and golden scales when her doubts returned. This couldn't last. Nothing did. People left. They betrayed you. And there had been so many in her life...

She made her decision. When the Green Knight woke, she would be gone.

So why couldn't she move? Why couldn't she leave him, leave her family, before they left her?

She'd do it. She would. Soon.

The drowsiness threatened to return as a sudden darkness fell. The sunlight had been swallowed up by swirling charcoal-colored clouds. Thunder roared.

There was no rain, only wind. Patience sensed that nature was gathering her power and fury.

"Green Knight," she whispered, rising. "Get up!"

His eyes flickered open.

"We have to get out of here!"

Something was coming. Patience felt it.

The Green Knight rose and walked forward. The heavy winds buffeted him. Patience felt them, too.

She studied the horizon, waiting for the danger to show itself. Suddenly, it rose up over the hill behind them and came screaming toward them.

What approached was *not* a thing of the earth. It had come from the heavens. A swirling gray mass with spidery tendrils of lightning flashing in its outer reaches. Caught up in its hungry embrace were shattered trees, jagged rock, mud, slime, and writhing, living *things*.

A twister!

Its base was thirty feet across, its top blotting out the sky.

The Green Knight roared defiantly to warn the twister away. Patience screamed at him to run but could no longer hear herself over the deafening roar of the winds that slammed at her.

The Green Knight blinked at the rushing wall of wind and fury heading right for him. Finally, he ran. Patience tried to stay beside him, but the twister cut a path between them.

Patience cut across the landscape. Tree trunks cracked and broke behind her. No matter where she ran, the twister followed.

The way before her was a confusion of sharp rises and a series of cracks and crevices. She recognized the area and realized that she'd been racing *away* from the Acrocanthosaurus encampment, away from home.

Her family was safe.

Patience had no idea if the Green Knight had escaped the twister or if he had been swallowed up by it.

No! she chided herself. *He is safe. He has to be!*

Lightning reached out and blasted a tree to her left. She ran until her legs burned and her chest stung. The twister almost had her! Worst of all, the way ahead was dangerous. Some of the cracks in the earth were only a few feet across and a yard deep. But others were chasms twenty yards across and fifty deep.

She saw four rises ahead, with three possible paths to take between them. She had to choose among the three paths, with no way of knowing where any of them would lead.

The twister dragged her arms back, and her claws were nearly pried open. *You're not getting it!* she thought, clutching the amber key tighter.

Then Patience did the last thing she would ever do in a game, praying this strategy would fake out her opponent. She chose the center path, put her head down, and ran for it!

The twister veered off, racing up the sharp rise to her right. A huge branch sailed at her like a javelin, missing her head by inches.

Patience wanted to stop and let the twister move ahead of her, but the constant shower of debris made that impossible. She had to keep running, dodging the shower of earth and rock.

The twister drove her on, into the open!

She saw the land ahead. It was flat. Once she was out there, she would be the tallest object around, and the twister would be on her again.

The narrow lane between the rises widened, and Patience heard the twister descend. It was no longer a force of nature.

She thought of the Green Knight and the way he had stood his ground and roared as the twister came right for him. As if it had been alive...

To Patience, the storm now had a face and a form. It was everyone and everything that had ever left her, or had forced her to leave.

Patience ran into the open and turned. But there was no face in the swirling funnel. Nothing that laughed triumphantly. The malevolent *thing* she'd been running from didn't really exist. This *was* a force of nature, nothing more.

Then the ground beneath her feet gave way. She howled as the twister came at her. Patience tumbled over the edge of a crevice she hadn't even seen. She struck the ground hard, even as earth and rock dropped on her, pinning her in place. Only her snout and one eye were exposed.

Lightning flashed and struck the earth, blinding her! She squeezed her eye shut as the breath was drawn from her lungs—

And the twister roared away.

Patience, practically buried, breathed hard for several moments.

An image of the key flashed in her mind. The frail, fragile key...

She could feel something in her palm, but she couldn't tell if the key was still in one piece. Slowly and carefully, she extracted herself from the loosely packed earth and examined the amber key.

A small piece had chipped off near the handle. Patience dug in the earth until she found it.

It can be fixed, she told herself.

Then she climbed out of the crevice and looked

around. The winds were still heavy, the sky a thick gray.

Patience tensed as she felt the pull of Ground Zero and realized that was where the storm was headed.

She ran toward Ground Zero, trying not to think about the Green Knight and home. Yet, a mournful feeling rose in her. It was the emotion of her inner dino, certain that she would never find her way back home.

But that wasn't *Patience's* problem. It wasn't!

Even so, the idea made her sad. So she paid close attention to odd landmarks that might help her host dino get home when this was over. It was a route she also wanted to learn in case their mission was a failure.

She followed the storm for several hours until she saw a jutting tree branch, perhaps the longest she'd ever seen. Now *that* was a landmark—

"Over here!" came a muffled voice. Patience narrowed her eyes and saw the branch *moving*.

Zane. The "landmark" was his long neck!

The brontosaur stood beside a copse of tall trees. Runt was playing at his feet. Mr. London was in one of the trees, trying to avoid the baby long-neck.

The teacher was scrambling along the swaying branches. "Did you get it? Did you?"

Patience held out the key. "A little piece broke off, but I've got that, too." Then she turned. "Look!"

The Hypsilophodon froze as he saw the storm's swirling winds form a funnel cloud.

The twister was back!

"Mr. L!" Patience yelled. "You've got to come down. Now!"

The teacher stared at the dark spiral, entranced.

"Zane, bring him down!" Patience commanded.

Zane thrust his head high into the branches and tapped Mr. London's flank until the teacher climbed onto his head.

"Going down," Zane whispered.

Patience accepted delivery of the quaking teacher. She held him in one arm, and he whimpered.

She looked at the trees ahead, focusing on one in particular. Its trunk was enormous, and its roots snaked into the ground in every direction.

"Over there!" Patience snarled. "Move it!"

The winds were terrible.

Zane led Runt toward the huge tree. Patience followed with Mr. London.

"I—I saw something like this on the Discovery Channel," Mr. London said.

Patience held him close. She wasn't going to lose any of them. Not to the twister. Not to whatever was waiting at Ground Zero. Not ever again.

She instructed Zane to wrap his front limbs around the base of the tree. Runt huddled close and seized one of Zane's legs. Zane lowered his bulk to help wedge the little dinosaur in place.

Patience looked at Mr. London. "Do you trust me?"

He nodded.

"Good." She pressed him up against Zane's left leg, then wrapped her little arms around it. Mr. London was wedged in tight. She grasped the amber key, afraid that it would shatter.

She could feel the twister pulling at her already.

"Zane's neck!" Mr. London gasped. "He has to anchor it under those roots!"

Patience understood. Zane's tail could twist and curl, but if his neck was forced to bend, it would break. There was another large tree just ahead. Its roots looped in and out of the ground like horse-shoes.

"Zane, are you listening?" Patience called. The twister was nearly upon them.

"R-roots?" he stammered.

"Slide your head and neck under them. Do it!"

Zane flattened himself, nearly burying Patience and Mr. London in the blubber that was his belly. He crouched low enough to slip his head and neck under the roots.

Mr. London was fighting against her.

"Can't *breathe,* crushing me—"

"Zane!" Patience yelled. "Your left leg! Move your left leg a couple of inches."

Patience stumbled forward, losing her grip. Mr. London scrambled out from underneath her just before she hit the ground. Zane's weight plopped down on her, pinning her in place.

Then the twister moved over them.

"I'll be good I'll be good..." Zane chanted.

Patience grabbed Mr. London. His little body didn't squirm against her anymore. She wondered if he'd passed out.

Zane's body was buffeted. Above them, branches shattered and flew off. Zane's incredible bulk was lifted up, his tail whipping frantically.

Patience held Zane's leg, keeping her grip loose enough not to crush the key or her teacher.

She saw Runt holding on, his neck pressed against the underside of Zane's belly, his feet off the ground. She was in the air, too. Her grip started to slip. She clamped her jaws on Zane's leg.

"Yow!" he yelled. She could hear his voice in her head.

She shifted her gaze to Mr. London and gasped.

The thing in her grip wasn't Mr. London. It was a log, a soggy log covered with leaves, a chunk of the debris carried by the twister!

Then she saw a tiny figure spinning in the air. A wailing rose up in her mind.

"Hellllllllllp meeeeeeeeeee!" the teacher pleaded.

Everyone leaves, Patience thought wildly.

Everyone—

    She hollered as the winds let up and Zane's body fell on her again, mashing her down. Patience broke free just in time to see the twister spiraling away, taking Mr. London with it.

BOB

Splashdown!

Bob London heard the roar of the twister moving off as he fought to keep himself from sinking beneath the water. He was dizzy and clung to a hollow tree branch until he felt better. Then he swam to shore.

He had no idea how long he'd ridden the twister. He'd blacked out several times. None of it mattered. He was alive!

As he swam, he smelled the fresh, clean tang of the water. A host of other smells came to him. There was life on the shore, but no threats that he could sense.

Ahead, he saw bright, fresh patches of green under a soft blue sky. It was beautiful.

Life was beautiful!

All the terror had gone. He had faced something greater than himself, a power that dwarfed even that of the M.I.N.D. Machine.

What he had just experienced was not something he read or theorized about. For once, he had been on the inside of an event. He wanted more!

He was hungry. Thirsty. Happy.

"I'm giddy!" Bob London yelled. "Giddy!"

He reached the shore and didn't think about taking careful mental notes or cataloguing the plants he saw. What mattered was the thrilling joy released within him.

Glorious. Just glorious.

He shook off the lake water and found a nice clearing where he could bask in the sun.

He dozed for an hour or two—and woke to high, chittering sounds. He rolled onto his back and rubbed his spine against a rock, scratching an itch.

This is like being at camp, he decided. *And I'm a happy camper!*

Then he saw four other Hypsilophodons eyeing him curiously. They chittered and chirped. Each was yellow and red.

"Hello!" Bob said.

They stood on their hind legs. He did the same.

"What do you do for fun around here?" Bob asked.

The tiny dinosaurs looked about suspiciously.

"Something I said?" Bob asked.

Suddenly, the ground thundered and shook!

Bob fell on his tail as sharp hisses came from every direction.

THREAT-THREAT-THREAT cried a voice within him. He saw vines fall from the trees nearby.

A band of gray-scaled dinosaurs emerged from the woods surrounding him. The sun glinted off their sharp teeth and claws. Bob recognized them at once.

Microvenators. Meat-eaters. They weren't much bigger than the Hypsilophodons, but they were deadly. Bob could sense their hunger. It burned in their dark eyes.

Another thundering footfall rumbled. A shadow draped the clearing.

Bob looked up to see the largest creature that had ever walked the earth. It was a long-neck, but far bigger than Zane. From the tip of its tail to the end of its snout, it was one hundred feet long. Its head was so high it almost disappeared from view.

The ground shook again. Then a gigantic scaly column with a single outthrust claw and a rough, callused pad loomed overhead. It was so big that Bob wondered if it could fit into his living room.

This isn't good, he thought.

He stood—frozen with all the others—as the dinosaur's foot came crashing down!

To be continued in
PLEASE DON'T EAT THE TEACHER!

#4

PLEASE DON'T EAT THE TEACHER!

by Scott Ciencin

Zane was trudging along the outskirts of a lush forest when Patience nudged him.

"Do you notice something?" she asked.

"If you're going to say, 'It's quiet, *too* quiet,' I promise I'll scream like I'm in a cheesy horror movie."

Patience hesitated. "But it is, isn't it?"

Zane hated to admit it, but it was. He looked around, scanning for predators.

Nothing. Not even—

"*Runt!*" Looking back along his flanks, Zane was startled to see that the baby bronto was gone. He turned to Patience. "I thought you were watching him! You let him run off?"

She shook her head. "I didn't *let* him do anything. You weren't paying attention, either."

Zane squeezed his eyes shut and banged his head against the trunk of a tree. "We've got to find him."

"Why?"

Zane's eyes narrowed. "He's family."

"Okay. I know his scent. This'll go faster if we're working together."

As they tracked the smaller dinosaur, the tingling, pleasant smell of fresh water rushed toward them. A river!

If Runt was lost, he would be drawn to the water.

Zane hurried ahead with Patience and crested a small rise. Below him, a small island sat in the middle of a wide river. On it, a large form frolicked among a host of smaller ones.

Runt!

"Hey, buddy!" Zane called. He happily headed down the slope, Patience not far behind.

As he entered the water, Zane thought he smelled something new. Something small and light and unfamiliar and—

HUNGRY-HUNGRY-HUNGRY

He looked back at Patience, and fear gripped him. A pair of nasty-looking dinosaurs raced at her from either side. Curved little sickle claws appeared from their feet.

Raptors.

"Patience, get in the water! Mr. London said raptors have fragile bodies—they won't be able to take the current!"

Patience stumbled toward the froth.

HUNGRY-HUNGRY-HUNGRY

Standing in the river, Zane looked ahead and saw a trio of raptors on the *other* shore.

Waiting.

#4
PLEASE DON'T EAT THE TEACHER!

COMING IN JULY 2000

#5

BEVERLY HILLS BRONTOSAURUS
by Scott Ciencin

HAS JUDGMENT DAY ARRIVED?

My name is J.D. "Judgment Day" Harms. At Wetherford Junior High, I was the baddest of the bad. No one messed with me if they knew what was good for them. But now I'm trapped back in time, in the body of a leaf-eating Apatosaurus. All around me are these meat-eaters, giving me this look like I'm their next Happy Meal. Stupid carnivores. They think I'm just another defenseless longneck. Boy, are *they* in for a surprise!

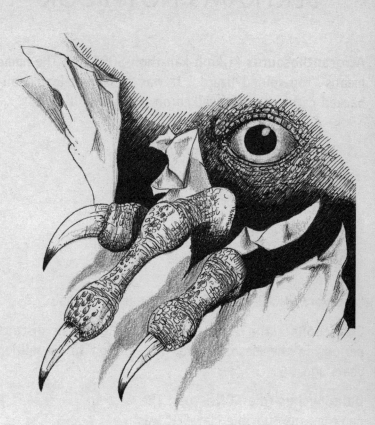

BERTRAM'S
NOTEBOOK

BERTRAM'S NOTEBOOK

Acrocanthosaurus (a-kroh-kan-thoh-SORE-us): The name means "top-spined lizard." It was a 39-foot-long, sail-backed carnivore that walked on its two hind legs.

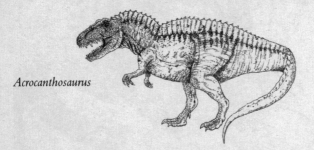

Acrocanthosaurus

Carnivores (KAR-nuh-vorz): Meat-eating animals.

Cretaceous (krih-TAY-shus): The last of three distinct periods in the Mesozoic Era, 145 million to 65 million years ago.

Deinonychus

Deinonychus (die-NON-i-kus): The name means "terrible claw." It was up to 10 feet long and had large fangs, a powerful jaw, muscular legs, and a retractable scythe-like claw on the second toe of each foot. Commonly known as "raptors," Deinonychus were fast and agile and usually hunted in packs to take down large prey.

Herbivores (HUR-bih-vorz): Plant-eating animals.

Hypsilophodon (hip-sih-LOH-foh-don): The name means "high ridge tooth." This dinosaur was a small herbivore, only about four to seven feet in length, but it was very quick. It walked on its two strong back legs.

Hypsilophodon

Iguanodon (ig-WHA-noh-don): The name means "iguana tooth." This was a large herbivore that varied in lengths up to about 30 feet and walked on its hind legs. Its five-fingered "hands" had a spiked thumb, three middle fingers with hooflike nails, and a fifth finger that could be used for grasping.

Iguanodon

Invertebrates (in-VUR-tuh-braytz): Animals without backbones, like jellyfish.

Mesozoic Era (mez-uh-ZOH-ik ER-uh): The age of dinosaurs, 245 million to 65 million years ago.

Microvenator (MYE-kroh-vi-NAY-tor): The name means "tiny hunter." It was a small carnivorous dinosaur that walked on its hind legs and had unusually long arms.

Microvenator

Nodosaurus (no-doh-SORE-us): The name means "node lizard." It was a large armored herbivore that walked on all fours and was related to Ankylosaurus.

Paleontologist (pay-lee-un-TAHL-uh-jist): A scientist who studies the past through fossils.

Pleurocoelus

Pleurocoelus (PLEW-roh-SEEL-us): The name means "hollow side." It was a large herbivore with a long neck and walked on all fours. It is commonly referred to as a "brontosaurus" and is the official state dinosaur of Texas.

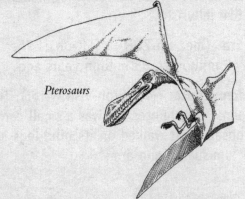

Pterosaurs

Pterosaurs (TER-uh-sorz): Sizable and varied flying reptiles.

Sauroposeidon (SORE-oh-POSI-don):
The name means "earthquake-god
lizard." It was recently discovered
in southeast Oklahoma. Considered
the largest dinosaur ever to walk
the earth, Sauroposeidon was a
long-neck that walked on all four legs,
weighed 60 tons, and stood 60 feet tall.
It was 100 feet in length.

Sauroposeidon

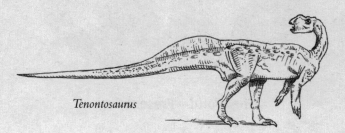

Tenontosaurus

Tenontosaurus (TEH-NON-toh-SORE-us): The name means
"sinew lizard." It was a large, horse-faced herbivore with
an average length of 24 feet. It could walk on either two
or four legs and could achieve great running speed if
given time to warm up. In a surprise attack by a predator, however, the Tenontosaurus might lose the chase
without time to reach its top speed.

Vertebrates (VUR-tuh-braytz): Animals with backbones,
such as fish, mammals, reptiles, and birds.

The World: The continents and the seas of the earth 112 million years ago were different from those in our present day. The inland sea was already through Canada and was starting to enter what would later be the United States. Mexico and parts of many southern states, including Arizona, Texas, Louisiana, Alabama, and Florida were under water. Parts of Asia were also under water. South America and Africa were still joined together. Australia had broken away from Africa.

The World—Present Day

The World—112 Million Years Ago

SCOTT'S FAVORITE DINO SITES

(and Bertram has them bookmarked, too!)

DINOSAUR INTERPLANETARY GAZETTE
www.dinosaur.org
This site has everything! You'll find up-to-date information on the newest and coolest dinosaurs (check out DNN, the Dinosaur News Network); plenty of links, jokes, quotes, interviews with authors (like me!) and paleontologists, and contests; and much, much more! The Gazette is the winner of 22 Really Kewl Awards and is recommended by the National Education Association.

DINOSAUR WORLD
www.dinoworld.net
A "nature preserve" for hundreds of awesome life-size dinosaurs, located in Plant City, Florida, between Tampa and Orlando. I've never seen anything like it! Check it out on the Net, then go see it for yourself!

DINOTOPIA
www.dinotopia.com
I'm the author of four Dinotopia digest novels, *Windchaser, Lost City, Thunder Falls*, and *Sky Dance*. Dinotopia is one of my favorite places to visit. This is the official Web site of James Gurney's epic creation.
Enter a world of wonder where humans and dinosaurs peacefully coexist. Ask questions of Bix, post messages to fellow fans, and be sure to let Webmaster Brokehorn know that Scott at DINOVERSE sent you!

PREHISTORIC TIMES
members.aol.com/pretimes
This Web site offers information about the premier magazine for dinosaur enthusiasts around the world—published by DINOVERSE illustrator Mike Fredericks. For dinosaur lovers, aspiring dinosaur artists, and more!

ZOOMDINOSAURS.COM
www.zoomdinosaurs.com
A terrific resource for students. Lots of puzzles, games, information for writing dinosaur reports, classroom activities, an illustrated dinosaur dictionary, frequently asked questions, and fantastic information for dinosaur beginners.

• AUTHOR'S SPECIAL THANKS •

Thanks to Denise Ciencin, M.A., National Certified Counselor, for her many valued and wonderful contributions to this novel. For their assistance in helping me to construct the world of Texas and Oklahoma 150 million years ago, thanks to paleontologists Louis L. Jacobs, Ph.D., Department of Geological Sciences, Southern Methodist University, Dallas, Texas; Professor Richard Cifelli, University of Oklahoma (leader of the team that found the Sauroposeidon); Bonnie Jacobs of Southern Methodist University, Dallas, Texas; and David Nicklin, Chief Geologist, Arco Oil, Plano, Texas.

Special thanks to Alice Alfonsi, my extraordinary editor, and all our friends at Random House, especially Kate Klimo, Kristina Peterson, Craig Virden, Georgia Morrissey, Andrew Smith, Daisy Kline, Amy Wells, Mike Wortzman, Kenneth LaFreniere, Artie Bennett, Jenny Golub, Christopher Shea, and Doby Daenger.

Final thanks to my incredible agent, Jonathan Matson.